Time Out

Time Out

How to Take a Year (or More or Less) Off without Jeopardizing Your Job, Your Family, or Your Bank Account

BONNIE MILLER RUBIN

W · W · NORTON & COMPANY
New York   London

The text of this book is composed in Times Roman, with display type set in
Clarendon. Composition and manufacturing by The Haddon Craftsmen, Inc.
Book design by Jacques Chazaud.

First Edition

Library of Congress Cataloging-in-Publication Data

Rubin, Bonnie Miller.
  Time out.

  Includes index.
  1. Leave of absence. 2. Leisure. 3. Time management. I. Title.
HD5255.R82 1987 640 87–5723

ISBN 0-393-02393-1

ISBN 0-393-30510-4 {PBK}

W. W. Norton & Company, Inc., 500 Fifth Avenue, New York, N. Y. 10110
W. W. Norton & Company Ltd., 37 Great Russell Street, London WC1B 3NU

1 2 3 4 5 6 7 8 9 0

To my parents,
    who taught me to dream

To David and Michael,
    proof that dreams do come true

CONTENTS

ACKNOWLEDGMENTS

This book started almost three years ago with a journey. Along the way, there have been a few people who have been with me every step:

My agent, Jeanne Hanson, who believed in this project from its inception.

My editor at W. W. Norton, Mary Cunnane, who saw possibilities where everyone else saw pie-in-the-sky. She never tired of shaping, refining, and polishing, her perseverance molding a rough manuscript to a finished book.

My copyeditor, Nancy Palmquist, who did an excellent job.

My dear friend, Linda Cosby, who not only lent me her Macintosh—before she even had a chance to take it out of the box—but provided me with computer expertise at all hours of the day and night. I could not have written *Time Out* without her generosity and indomitable spirit.

Wayne Miller of Howard Zucker and Associates and Louis Lichtenfeld of Dean Witter Reynolds Inc., who provided expert financial advice and never tired of dumb questions—or, if they did, were too polite to say so.

Beverly Kees, my editor in chief at the *Post-Tribune,* my mentor and my friend, for time to work on the book, even though my seniority in my new position could be measured in weeks, not years. Any professional success I've achieved can be attributed to her sound judgment, sure hand, and unshakable faith.

No list of acknowledgments would be complete without thanks to family and friends who kept me in everything from babysitters to paperclips. They are the backbone of this project.

"One of the symptoms of an approaching nervous breakdown is the belief that one's work is terribly important."

BERTRAND RUSSELL

PROLOGUE

It all started innocently enough. Six professionals, all between the ages of 32 and 45, playing "What would you do if you only had one wish" over dinner.

"I'd go back to school and study music," said the pediatrician.

"I'd read all the books that have been gathering dust on the shelves for umpteen years," said the attorney.

"I'd set up my easel and paint Cape Cod sunsets," said the accountant, with a sigh loud enough to be heard at the next table. By dessert, we were all thoroughly depressed.

I was struck by the humbleness of everyone's wishes. No Rolls Royces, Park Avenue penthouses, or Lear jets—just the gift of time.

"Something is wrong here," I said to my husband on the way home. "What have we become, when reading is regarded as some decadent pleasure?"

I knew what I had become: an overwhelmed journalist/wife/mother, who, at age 33, was not so much living as "coping." From the time the alarm went off at 5:30 A.M. until I collapsed in bed some eighteen hours later, my day was tightly scripted. No time for friendships, for hobbies, for choices. No time *period*. For the first time, that seemed like a terribly high price to pay.

For me to daydream about being on a campus, a beach—anywhere but the office—was alarmingly out of character. Journalism isn't a job, it's a calling. Reporters may complain constantly and threaten to chuck it all (usually every day around deadline) but, the truth is, most of us are passionate about what we do. Ever since I was nine, when I started the "Fourth Grade Fighter" (I forget what exactly I was crusading against), I wanted to spend my life in a newsroom—and after almost fifteen years in the business, I still came in early, stayed late, and went into the office on weekends to "catch up on paperwork."

That was precisely the problem. I had clung to the myth that as soon as I finished that story (or went through the mail, or returned those phone calls) I would get around to some time for me. But tomorrow, there was always another story, another stack of mail, another fistful of phone messages. Like some kind of Pac-Man, my job devoured every available moment until there was no time for anything else. A vacation would just be a Band-Aid. I needed enough time to restore balance to my lopsided life. I needed enough distance to get a perspective on work. Three months later, the solution came in the form of a crushing rejection.

I had applied for a fellowship at the University of Michigan, which offers annually a year of mid-career rejuvenation and a generous stipend to twelve journalists. Competition for the fellowships is keen, and after completing lengthy application forms, writing weighty essays, and appearing before a judging committee, I was selected as a finalist.

However, for the first time in the program's history, budget cuts made it necessary to reduce the number of fellowships from twelve to ten—and one of those axed slots was mine. I was hit by a tidal wave of disappointment. When September rolled around, it would not be me who was packing up the U-Haul and heading for the solitude of ivy-covered walls and walnut-paneled libraries. Instead, I would be sitting at the same desk, regurgitating the same stories, and fighting the same battles that I had for seven previous Septembers.

"You can do it," said an encouraging colleague, as I stared at my blank computer screen. But I couldn't do it. I was exhausted and ground down by the routine. In the last five years, I had been through a newspaper merger, two rounds of layoffs, and three bosses. I had channeled every ounce of energy into a business that cranked out a new product every twenty-four hours; I had shoveled all my creativity into an insatiable machine that ate everything I fed it—and then roared for more. And I was caught in the crossfire of a managerial power struggle. Finally, as a features writer, I had no clout to do the kinds of stories I wanted to do. (Woodward and Bernstein never had to find a new angle on "back to school" fashions.) In fact, I had no clout, period.

My precious labor of love had escalated into an oppressive burden.

When I lost that fellowship, I couldn't just shrug my shoulders and tackle my work with business-as-usual zeal. Once the door had opened a crack and I had caught a glimpse of a world blissfully free of alarm clocks, interoffice memos, and political infighting, I couldn't slam it shut and pretend that it never existed.

What started as a wistful daydream became a burning desire. I searched for another fellowship, but by this time all the deadlines had passed. I even offered to raise the necessary funds for the Michigan program but was politely discouraged. Crazily, when a friend landed in bed for three months following a car accident, I fantasized that the same thing would happen to me. Then I thought, why should a serious injury be the only way to recharge my batteries? Why does the corporate world give its blessing to take time off when you're sick, but never when you're well?

If management wasn't going to just hand over a block of time—for growth, for knowledge, for rest, for relaxation—then it was up to me to *make* it happen, to do whatever I needed to do, to convince whomever I needed to convince that a sabbatical was indeed a noble endeavor. I didn't have the slightest idea of where to start, but there was one thing I knew with absolute certainty: I was no longer willing to surrender all my waking hours to my employer. I couldn't shake this uneasy feeling that I was missing something. That while I was putting in fifty or sixty hours a week at the office, life was passing me by.

Perhaps you're taking that same kind of inventory. Goals that were once important now seem meaningless. Being named salesman of the year or becoming chairman of the board by the time you're 40 seems like a hollow reward when compared to the sacrifices you've had to make. Then the proverbial lightbulb goes off and you realize that you've been following someone else's agenda. That what you *really* want has nothing to do with titles or awards. I wasn't concerned about dying without having won a Pulitzer Prize. Or even just dying. I was concerned with *not having lived.* I had spent most of my adult life writing about other people's adventures. Now I was ready for some of my own.

This is what *Time Out* is about: doing something for yourself. It is about taking a sabbatical—for a couple of months, a summer, a year, or even longer—whether it's to learn the cello, write a screenplay, or hike the Himalayas. At its core is the belief that everyone—not just university professors—should have time for reflection without jeopardizing everything they have worked so hard to accomplish.

In an era when the workplace is constantly being redefined, a sabbatical is a ticket off an endless treadmill, and one that is being increasingly used by career-oriented professionals. (While blue-collar workers are just as in need of "time out" as anyone else, the advice in this book is directed primarily towards the "fast-trackers.")

None of the people who took time out and whom I interviewed for this book were dilettantes or goof-offs. On the contrary, they were responsible, conscientious, tax-paying citizens who just wanted to wean themselves off the work addiction—at least temporarily. Some used their hiatus to recapture opportunities they thought were irretrievably lost, like backpacking through Europe or sailing to the Caribbean. Others traveled no farther than their basement darkroom or their local college campus. All were eager to flex other muscles, to exercise other parts of their brain, to put their careers on hold while they pursued other interests.

Can you? You bet. I'm going to show you how to recognize when it's time to put some distance between you and the office, how to negotiate a leave with your employer, how to come up with the cash you'll need (therefore reducing your dependency on your paycheck), how to rent your house or apartment and find new quarters, how to store your car—even how to minimize reentry shock when you return. This is a handbook, but it is a head- and heartbook as well.

I want to give you more than inspirational rhetoric. I want to give you a blueprint to lead you to the most precious commodity of all—time. The idea of a sabbatical opens up possibilities that you may not have thought were attainable for years—perhaps not even until retirement—and it puts them in your hands *right now*.

I know because I did it.

When the fellowship program fell through, I decided not to let the chance for a respite vanish along with it. The only difference was that instead of seeing Michigan, my family and I would see the world—and we would foot the bill ourselves.

Any sane person could see that my husband and I had no business considering anything more ambitious than a week in Florida. We had a five-year-old son, a thirty-year mortgage, two cars, a lawnmower, a snowblower, a goldfish, and a platoon of G.I. Joes. It was pure suburbia—hardly the kind of life that lent itself to exploring the ruins of ancient Greece.

But then, we had always done everything by the book: school, job, marriage, parenthood (in that order). Anyone who probed our pasts would find no gaps, no unaccounted-for summers or semesters spent "finding ourselves" while living out of a van. We had never played the part of the rebel, for fear of alienating our parents—both corporate and biological. Indeed, I had graduated college on a Saturday and started work on a Monday—and, at the time, was proud of it. Now that seemed just plain sad.

The pace wasn't much different a decade later, when we became parents and I returned to work before my son was four months old. The first day back I was assigned a new beat and a new boss. Eventually, my husband David, an architect, and I became adept at holding it all together—even if it was with baling wire and rubber bands. There was no slack in the schedule. My day seemed like one long surge of adrenaline—from dropping off our son, Michael, at the sitter to making sure my story was in on time to standing in line at the supermarket to rushing through the bedtime ritual. I felt obliged to turn every increment of time into something productive. (I once used a three-car accident to clean out my glove compartment.) But isn't that the goal? achievement? productivity? excellence?

"What would you think of spending a year traveling?" I asked David one night between the soup and the salad. "I'm sure I could get a leave of absence."

Actually, I lied. I had no idea how my employer felt about personal leaves. But if they had been willing to give me a year to study in Michigan, why not a year to wander the streets of Jerusalem, Paris, and Rome?

I knew David's weakness. Over the years, I've seen the spring in his step as he walks through an airport, the youthful exuberance at the prospect of even the most dreary locale. In 1973, he was accepted to the Peace Corps and turned it down for marriage and career, a fact he recalled wistfully every now and then. Is it possible for an opportunity to come around a second time?

This regret—along with his growing disenchantment with architecture and a feeling of being underutilized, unappreciated, and lost in the shuffle of a big firm—made David leap at the prospect of a sabbatical. But he is also immensely practical. If David left his job, he could shop his portfolio around to another half-dozen firms in Minneapolis without ever changing zip codes. But, because there is only one other major metropolitan daily in the Twin Cities, if I burned my bridges at the office it could either mean leaving Minnesota or leaving newspapers, a choice neither of us were willing to make. I didn't want to close the door on journalism—I just wanted a chance to step off the merry-go-round for a while. But for me to do that freely, I needed the safety net of having the job waiting for me when I returned.

"If you can get a leave, then let's do it," he said.

I had just cleared the first hurdle: a willing spouse. As long as I knew that this was a joint venture, then everything else—money, house, in-laws—could be worked out.

From that moment on we laid the groundwork to spend a year abroad. Rather than going through a briefcase stuffed with work, I used my evenings to work out a budget, draw up timetables, write away for information. I started stockpiling soap, shampoo, and toothpaste, just in case we ended up somewhere primitive. Even the mundane concerns of a leave were exhilarating because they were *my* concerns. For a decade and a half, I had put my career above everything else. Now it was time to lavish some of that same time and energy on myself and my family.

After much deliberation, we settled on Israel as our primary destination. We'd always had an intense interest in the Middle East, and we decided to live on a kibbutz—a communal agricultural settlement—where volunteers work in exchange for room and board. It was a good fit for several reasons. With its sunshine, healthy environment, and emphasis on cooperation, we knew that this was a place where our son would thrive. Besides stretching our travel dollar, this unique arrangement would allow us to really interact with Israelis, rather than just being American tourists on an extended holiday. Also, most Israelis speak English, a major selling point considering that neither of us had language skills beyond menu French.

But my boss still held the trump card. At the *Minneapolis Star and Tribune,* where there is particular reverence for the chain of command, I decided to ignore corporate etiquette and address my memo to the editor in chief. (This was too important to risk being squashed by some middle manager.) He was not only the chief executive officer of the newsroom, but a father with three young children. Hoping that if I couldn't sell him on professionalism, maybe I could appeal to his paternal instincts, I stressed in my letter, not only that this leave would give me a wealth of knowledge that would serve me well as a journalist, but that it would also give me some much-needed family time. For good measure, I threw in that this was an opportunity to grow healthier—physically, mentally, and spiritually.

The answer was yes.

I'm not sure which of those points struck the right chord; maybe it was merely the prospect of saving my salary. I'd like to think that it was an acknowledgment of my dedication, but I never asked and he never volunteered. In fact, there was very little feedback—from him or my other superiors—which, I realize now, was one of the reasons why I was seeking a leave in the first place.

Whatever the motivation, my memo was returned with a single word—"approved"—gloriously scrawled across the top.

I know what you're thinking: even with a guarantee that your desk will be waiting when you return, you will probably still worry that you are going to undo years of hard work: Am I committing professional suicide? Will someone move in on my turf while I'm gone? What if someone else gets that promotion I've been coveting? Quite simply, you won't be at the table when they cut up the pie.

No one ever takes a sabbatical without being frightened. I can't tell you that all your personal goals will be reached, that all your plans will go without a hitch, or even that you will accomplish everything you hoped to do. But there is one thing I can guarantee: that you will never have to wonder what *could* have been.

The test of my commitment came exactly one week before departure. A very attractive job offer and a chance to work for a much-respected editor caused me some last-minute soul searching. But in the final analysis, there were no advancements my career could offer that were as seductive as the adventure I had planned. I had been traveling down the well-worn, predictable path; now it was time to take the other fork in the road.

When we arrived at Lod Airport in Tel Aviv on New Year's Day, 1985, I had no idea what lay before us. Unknown to us then were the friendships we made, the lessons learned, the emotions stirred. I was uncertain about many things, but our decision to take time out was not one of them. When I caught my first glimpse of the Mediterranean, the months of intense planning—of searching for a renter, of enforced austerity, of endless "to do" lists— seemed like a small price to pay for the months of leisure that stretched ahead.

Eight months later—six in Israel, two in Europe—we returned with memories of planting trees and irrigating crops, of hiking the Swiss Alps and paddling Amsterdam's canals, of triumphing over the tyranny of the clock and the calendar. We returned with a contentment that comes from having dreams and seeing them come true.

INTRODUCTION
The Need for
Sabbaticals

Phyllis Jones, an American Indian and an operations manager at Wells Fargo Bank in San Francisco, left her job for three months to learn Navajo rug weaving on an Arizona reservation.

Charles Gusewell, a columnist for the *Kansas City Star,* spent six months writing his column from Paris.

Richard C. Csaplar, a partner in the law firm of Csaplar & Bok, left Boston for a year to be an adviser to the Supreme Court of Afghanistan.

In the three years I spent researching this book, I also met a Chicago clergyman who left his congregation to be a congressional fellow and a Los Angeles record producer who spent two years on a sailboat. The people who had taken sabbaticals were as diverse a group of professionals—living out every type of Walter Mitty fantasy—as you could possibly imagine; yet the results were curiously similar. They all returned with their batteries recharged, outlooks refreshed, and a zeal for sabbaticals that borders on the evangelical.

Not too long ago, the sabbatical was a privilege reserved for members of academia. The word conjured up images of a tweedy, pipe-smoking professor who had suffered through seven years of freshman English and was now getting his just rewards.

To qualify for a sabbatical today, no longer must you be a teacher or even a long-term employee; nor must you spend your time doing something even remotely work related. Throughout the country, people in all kinds of jobs, in all sizes of companies are discovering that it is possible to pursue all types of activities—from sailing the Caribbean to writing a screenplay—and still find their jobs waiting for them when they return.

Not only is it possible, but it is a movement that is picking up steam as an increasing number of companies recognize the value of the sabbatical in recruiting and retaining talented people. Linda Marks, a spokesman for New Ways to Work, a San Francisco research firm that has studied the trend, observes: "It's the benefit of the '90s. People are demanding more choices throughout their lives on how their work time can be arranged; that it doesn't have to be an all-or-nothing proposition; that it should complement rather than dominate other rewarding life endeavors."

For some companies, the '90s are already here. About fourteen percent of the nation's companies offer sabbaticals as part of their employee benefit programs. Among them are Time, Inc., Rolm Computers, McDonald's, and Moog, Inc. It is an innovation—like flex-time, job sharing, and paternity leave—offered by enlightened companies who know that meeting the needs of a constantly changing workforce is one way to increase productivity, enhance creativity, and instill loyalty.

While it may sound like the latest business fad, the concept of the sabbatical has its roots in the Old Testament. Sabbatical occurred every seven years and was a time when land and vineyards lay fallow and all debts were forgiven. In short, it was an opportunity to take stock and wipe the slate clean.

Those objectives are just as relevant today for Fortune 500 corporations and for small businesses—and not just for those at the pinnacle of the organizational chart. At Time, Inc., for example, all employees with ten years of service—whether they are columnists or custodians—may take a six-month leave at fifty percent salary for "growth and discovery."

"The reason we have the policy is that we want people to

rejuvenate themselves," said Ann Fitzgerald, benefits manager for the magazine group. "This is a very high-pressure business and long stretches without a break do nothing for the company and nothing for the employees. We want them to get out of the office and do their own thing, to return younger and healthier. And if that means lying on the beach, that's okay with us."

But few people are fortunate enough to work for companies that are willing to underwrite a tan. What about the rest of us who crave growth and discovery?

Of the seventy-five professionals whom I interviewed for this book, only three worked for companies that offered paid sabbaticals. The rest did it by themselves, for themselves, accomplishing the same goal by salting away their paychecks and negotiating time off with their employers. They acknowledge the tradeoffs, but they revel in the gains. "I was building something more important than a résumé or portfolio," said Mark Ugowski, a Palm Beach architect. "I was building me."

Just a few years ago, such comments would have raised eyebrows among ambitious, career-oriented professionals schooled in power dressing, power lunching, everything but power loafing.

Now the pendulum appears to be swinging the other way. Maybe it hit you while you were standing on a crowded bus on a sweltering afternoon or when you lied about a doctor's appointment in order to see your kid make his theatrical debut as a pilgrim in the Thanksgiving play. Or when you ran two red lights to get to the airport for a business trip—and then spent the next three hours sitting on the runway. Or when you worked all weekend on a project—only to find out on Monday morning that it had been postponed indefinitely. Or when you got the word that, after ten years of being groomed for division vice president, the division was being eliminated—and your coveted position along with it.

If you listen carefully, you can hear the corporate anthem—once sung with fervor—now being replaced by Peggy Lee's mournful tune, "Is that all there is?"

The signs of the diminished appetite for the fast track are everywhere. Personnel directors report that there is a greater interest among employees in reducing the amount of hours spent on

the job. Working part-time, for example, once thought to be the
kiss of death to a career, is becoming more common among professionals. Employees are turning down transfers and promotions
that mean more prestige and money but less leisure time. At salary
reviews, corporate stars are pressing for Fridays off or the freedom
to work from home rather than a raise.

No less an authority on the fast track than *Esquire* has not
only identified the trend, but has given it a name, "Cooling Out."
In a recent column, Editor Phillip Moffit described several men
who left enormously successful careers to pursue other interests.

"What I think is starting to occur is not a phenomenon of
failure, but of success. For it is the success these men have enjoyed
that has allowed them the opportunity to switch careers or simply
take time off in mid-life. Part of this success is, of course, financial.
But the most important element of all is psychological. These are
people with the strong self-image necessary to maintain an identity
without the prop of a career or a professional label: Doctor, Lawyer, Businessman."

Suddenly, the luxury of having a second cup of coffee in the
morning and lingering over the newspaper or driving out to the
country to see the leaves change color on an autumn afternoon
seems far more important than the office. You feel there are loftier
goals than placating a temperamental client or making your year-
end sales quota.

"A lot more of these people in their 30s and 40s are far more
introspective than we were," said Robert Lear, former board
chairman of the F&M Schaefer Corporation and a visiting professor at Columbia University's Business School. "They're more concerned about things such as self-fulfillment and personal choices.
They feel as if they've missed something."

Many of them have. "I came of age at a time when people *did*
things," said a 38-year-old Wall Street banker. "When I went to
college in the early '70s, everyone was involved—in human rights,
environmental groups, the arts. There was a high premium placed
on being a participant. Now my job leaves me too exhausted to
be anything but a spectator. The line between work and leisure has
totally vanished. Everyone I know works on the weekends and

does paperwork at home, not because they can't live without a BMW or a Gold Card, but because *that's what's expected.* If you're not interested in making that kind of contribution to the company, there are plenty of people who are. Sure, I would love to be a Big Sister or serve on the board of my neighborhood association, to be a whole person again rather than a caricature, but it's just not my time."

Such yearnings were expressed to me time and again, usually with the disclaimer, "I love my job but . . ." The frustration was almost palpable: of being way beyond dues paying, but too far from retirement; of the well running dry, but no oasis in sight.

A sabbatical can be that oasis. After single-mindedly devoting ten, fifteen, twenty years to your career—longer, if you count the years in school—it is a vehicle that can let you recoup some of what you've missed.

"In this country, we grow up with the idea that there are three distinct stages in our lives," said Richard Bolles, author of the job-hunter's bible, *What Color Is Your Parachute?*, and an enthusiastic supporter of extended leaves.

"We believe that when you're young, you study; when you're an adult, you work; and when you're old, you retire. It's what I call the three boxes of life and we are taught to take them in huge chunks. Today, however, people are increasingly discontented with these boxes—and a sabbatical is a way of mixing them up. It offers more than a breather from the daily grind. It enables a person to pursue his personal interests throughout his adult life while at the same time advancing his career, so he doesn't arrive at retirement feeling utterly useless. It gets people to examine the purpose of work, to ask themselves a lot of tough questions, like "What is it that I really want to be doing? What is it that I want to accomplish before I die?"

Srully Blotnick, a New York business psychologist and author, finds great value in this kind of self-assessment, particularly when it's done in mid-career.

"Ideally, the best time to take time off is between the ages of 30 and 45 because you have a better sense of who you are and what you want. Your 20s is when you should be acquiring experience, when you need to be banged around in the working world to find out what you like and what you don't like. And beyond age 45, it's just too risky. A lot of older managers leave only to find someone who is ten years younger, better trained, and better educated sitting in their chairs. But by the time you've reached your 30s and early 40s, you've honed your skills and can view your profession with some perspective. You recognize that your work life is one-third over and you don't want to waste the remaining two-thirds you have left."

While many leave-takers fit Blotnik's profile, there is no magic number—when your budget, your career, your relationships, your home, and your horoscope all converge at a precise point on the great chart of life. In my research, I found leave-takers who ranged in age from mid-20s to early 50s. Another common thread that united them all was that they were self-starters with strong convictions, with the vigor and self-confidence to throw themselves out of the nest. Said Blotnik: "It's too easy to be a drone, to be in it just for the paycheck. If you aren't in a job that you would essentially do for free, you're going to be very unhappy over the long haul."

A sabbatical differs from a vacation, not only in length, but in purpose. It is not dropping out, but an opportunity to stretch a whole new set of muscles and exercise other parts of your brain.

Actually, the late Eli Goldston, president of a Boston-based energy firm and the man credited with pioneering the sabbatical concept, believed that professionals would benefit from not one, but three extended leaves during the course of a career. Goldston envisioned a company that offered a structured sabbatical at age 35, when the leave-taker would do community or government service or further his education; an unrestricted sabbatical at age 50; and another at age 62 to ease the transition into retirement.

Many companies have offered social service sabbaticals, during which employees teach at universities or work for nonprofit organizations, while still being paid by their employers. Only during the last fifteen years or so have a significant number of companies offered the kind of no-strings-attached sabbaticals that Goldston recommended.

At the forefront of the trend are the Silicon Valley companies, such as Rolm Corporation in Santa Clara, California, which initiated the program in 1974. That's when former chairman Ken Oshman wanted to take some time off, so he made the company-paid sabbatical the most attractive facet of Rolm's benefit package. For every six years of service, each employee gets three months off at full pay (or, if desired, six weeks off at double pay).

"As a company, we were in on the ground floor," said Larry Chamberlin, company spokesman. "It's one of our most popular benefits and one that helps us keep—as well as attract—quality people. This is an extremely competitive business and we are fortunate to have top-notch people who give that extra ounce of productivity every day, who can bring new approaches to problem-solving. When you do that for six or seven years, you need more than a couple weeks' vacation. You need a real break. We are certain that this benefit is special enough to attract special people."

At Tandem Computer, Inc., another high-tech company, in Cupertino, California, employees are entitled to a fully-paid, six-week leave for every four years of service. The New York law firm of Otterbourg, Steindler, Houston & Rosen permits six-month paid sabbaticals twenty years after law school graduation. At McDonald's, full-time employees working in corporate and regional offices are entitled to ten weeks off with full pay after ten years on the job. The compensation may differ, but the idea is the same: you get time off and the company gets an energetic employee in return, and a great recruitment tool to boot.

Other companies have adopted variations on the sabbatical theme. Since 1971, IBM has allowed employees to take social service leaves, with full IBM pay, to volunteer at nonprofit community organizations.

More than 700 IBMers have been loaned to local groups and another 500 to educational institutions through the faculty loan program. Xerox, Control Data, Hewlett-Packard, and Wells Fargo are other companies that, while not offering sabbaticals as an across-the-board-entitlement, do offer them to selected employees.

At Wells Fargo, for example, applicants for one of the few company-sponsored "personal growth leaves" make their proposals to a formal committee. Over the years, participants have studied sculpture at the Academie des Beaux Arts in Paris, the culture of the South Pacific at the University of Hawaii, and bonsai gardening in Japan.

"A personal growth leave should be something you love to do, but can't accomplish because you're working," said Nancy Thompson, company spokesperson. "Before you leave, we want to see your specific goals and hear why it is important that they are fulfilled. We want to see photos of your Indian rugs or hear the piano concerto you were composing or read the children's book you were writing. We take our responsibility very seriously. We want to make sure it is going to someone who will appreciate and cherish the opportunity."

Then there are companies that offer little or no financial support, but place great emphasis on creating an open, innovative climate; where new ideas are more apt to be met with a "let's" rather than "let's not"; where performance is calculated in terms of output and contributions, rather than the old formulas of number of hours worked and sick days taken.

"Our product is technology, and there is some question whether you can do research in a straightjacket environment," said Alex Tillman, an administrative assistant at Bell Laboratories, which has a liberal track record on granting unpaid personal leaves. "The results speak for themselves. We have a very productive staff, with patents and Nobel Prizes to their credit. We try to work with the employee rather than against him and, in exchange, there is a lot of creativity that flows through this place."

But talking to people who already have sabbatical programs is like preaching to the converted. To some, they will be viewed as the height of narcissim: one more me-generation self-indulgence, on a par with mink bedspreads and caviar by the pound. "I have a hard time working up the proper sympathy for today's executive," said a retired executive of a hotel chain. "Not only did we have a depression and a world war to contend with, but we were not nearly as well compensated."

But, depression and war notwithstanding, health and business experts agree that these are indeed trying times.

Consider:

• Today's business world has galloped off at a speed greater than anything we have ever seen. No previous generation has had to face the foreign competition, the hostile takeovers, the mergers that can eliminate hundreds of jobs in the blink of an eye. Insecurity is rampant and no one is immune.

• The trend towards leaner organizations means fewer opportunities at the top. An abundance of talented people and a shortage of slots means a lot of careers are going to plateau sooner.

• No previous generation had to face constantly changing technology or worry about its long-term effects. (By 1990, at least half of the U.S. work force will be using some type of computer at work.)

• Previous generations did not have a drug culture so pervasive that employees needed to be tested as a condition of employment, or live in a time when so many countries had an atomic bomb at their disposal.

• No previous generation has been so inundated with information, leaving us no choice but to "sink or skim." We are asked to be Renaissance men and women in an age when that is no longer possible.

• Researchers—once reluctant to associate stress with vulnerability to disease—have collected evidence that is hard to ignore. The Framingham (Massachusetts) Heart Study, which studied a control group for twenty-five years, linked stress (including an unsupportive boss, no job mobility, and suppressed hostility) with premature heart disease when combined with other factors, such as hypertension, high cholesterol, and/or smoking.

• For all the talk about leisure time, America is a nation of workaholics. According to a recent *Wall Street Journal*/Gallup poll, which surveyed 720 executives, seventy-six percent reported that they worked fifty hours a week or more. We are enamored with the concept of lifelong education, yet neither the U.S. nor Canada has followed the lead of many European countries

(France, Germany, Sweden, Italy, Austria, Belgium, and Yugo-slavia) of instituting a legal right for time off to study. That means that an employee can take an educational leave and is guaranteed a job when he returns. While many of these programs are self-funded, some employers participate in a payroll deduction program, so the money is there when it is needed.

(In 1974, at its 59th session, the International Labor Organization adopted Convention 140, which recommends that paid educational leave be a matter of national policy among its members. The United Nations Educational Scientific and Cultural Organization (UNESCO) has also encouraged implementation of educational leaves.)

• Perhaps greatest of all, previous generations did not feel so torn by the demands of home and career. Today, only ten percent of all American households fit the 1950s mold of father as bread-winner and milk-and-cookie mother. Nearly half of all mothers with children under twelve months of age are in the work force, yet many employers have yet to come to terms with that fact. Who stays home when your kid gets sick or the sitter cancels? Who rushes home in the middle of the day when you get a call that Johnny has a 102-degree temperature? The pressure of keeping employee and parental roles separate and distinct adds an element of stress to many lives that could not have been predicted even twenty years ago.

Women are not the only ones sensitive to family issues. There are an increasing number of men who are pushing for paternity leaves and other ways to spend more time with their young children. And at the other end of the spectrum loom the responsibilities for the care of elderly parents, responsibilities that command the attention of many middle-aged children, regardless of gender.

Take all those elements and turn up the dial. Add Federal Express, red-eye flights, and car phones so you can conduct business at sixty-five miles per hour, and you can see why this is a generation left drained and depleted.

Some management consultants say the benefits of a sabbatical are overrated, that they are no more than a perk—and an expensive one at that. At many law firms, for example, the firm must not only absorb the departing employee's salary, but the loss of the revenues he would generate. When a firm has to pay for three or four concurrent salaries, the costs become prohibitive.

It isn't only the economics that present problems, say the detractors. Sabbaticals clash head-on with America's work ethic. Oh sure, those laid-back, high-tech California companies may offer them, but they don't work if you're turning out cereal or soap or bleach. Spokesmen for Proctor and Gamble, Bechtel, Clorox, and General Mills were unanimous in their objection that a leave would put key players too far outside the mainstream of business. They may return ready to get back into the game, but by that time the game may have changed.

"Teachers can take sabbaticals because the freshman algebra class will be the same this year and next year and the year after that, but the business world is too volatile," said Lowell Cohn, a former vice president for a Madison Avenue advertising agency, who walked away from money and prestige and eventually started the Biofeedback Center in Manhattan. His experience makes him uniquely qualified to play devil's advocate. "When an important player is away, clients get nervous, so bosses get nervous—and if your boss is nervous that doesn't do much for your career.

"If you want to thrive in an organization, you have to be on the home team. That means being the kind of guy who will be on twenty-four-hour call, the kind who works at the office all night, will take a cab home to shower and change and will jump back in the cab and do it all over again. All this talk about employers wanting healthy, balanced employees rather than one-dimensional corporate zombies sounds very nice, but it is, to a certain extent, lip service. What a company wants and what it says it wants are not necessarily the same thing."

Abraham Zaleznik, a professor at the Harvard Business School, questions the effectiveness of sabbaticals and the message they convey. "We're telling employees that their reward for good work is that they don't have to work. It encourages people to be takers, not givers," said Zaleznik, who himself took a two-year leave to write a book—which he completed in one.

"The most liberal employment practices in the world don't get people what they want—which is respect and self-esteem; that only comes from contributions."

What do companies want? Obviously, only you know your corporate culture. Is it a traditional environment, where a high premium is placed on conformity, where marching to the beat of a different drummer is seen as an act of treason? Or is it an environment that recognizes that employees may be most productive when they can coordinate their work life with other needs outside the office?

What do you want? Again, only you can assess your needs—and what it will take to satisfy those needs. Is it leisure, friends, recreation, independence, and challenge? Is it security, money power, and prestige?

To the leave-takers I interviewed, the answer was unanimous and passionate: They wanted time and were willing to do just about anything to get it. Each birthday released another surge of urgency, a feeling of "Oh, my God. I'm never going to be a brain surgeon or a ballerina or hit a home run in the World Series or give my Oscar acceptance speech—the one I've been practicing in the bathroom mirror since I was 12." The realization creates a burning desire to tackle the things that are still attainable, whether it is pounding out the Great American Novel, a canoe trip through the Canadian wilderness, or spending time with people we love.

"One Sunday morning, I saw this beautiful young woman standing in the hallway and I realized it was one of my daughters," said Charles Gusewell, the *Kansas City Star* columnist. "An eyeblink before she had been in her crib; an eyeblink later she would be off doing something that had absolutely nothing to do with me. This [the year abroad] was my way of doing something to stop the ferociously turning hands of the clock."

A leave cannot stop the clock, but it can slow it down, because—perhaps for the first time in your life—you're taking time off to fulfill your goals—not your parents' or your employer's—but *yours.*

Time Out

My sabbatical gave me an opportunity to do something I had always wanted to do, but never managed to find the time for—keeping a journal. Entries start below and appear throughout the book.

January 5, 1985

Our apartment is an Israeli version of the college dorm: two rooms and a kitchenette. But despite our spartan accommodations, there is the luxury of time. At home, even weekends are marred by obligations. Here, there are no meals to shop for, prepare, and clean up after. No car to repair, no yard to maintain. Even the laundry is done for you.

Today Michael and I explored the mountain behind our apartment. I buried some money in the dirt and told him about an old pirate who never returned for his treasure. He was delighted when he dug up some nickels. I could have done that in our backyard. Why didn't I? At home I'm always saying, "Hurry up!" Here it doesn't matter, because there's nowhere I have to be.

January 12, 1985

Michael is definitely a calmer, more cooperative, and less combative child. I love the changes that I'm seeing in him after just one week. It's funny—we're not spending that many more hours together, it just seems that way because there are fewer distractions. When I'm with him, I'm really with him and not thinking about the office or getting to the bank before it closes or what I'm going to make for dinner. I feel as if I've already swept away a lot of life's clutter. The pace is making all of us gentler people. When did Michael ever say, "I need someone to cuddle up with me"?

January 14, 1985

Competition—one of the most tiresome aspects of the newsroom—is unavoidable. You can't get away from it—even on a kibbutz, where everyone has the same possessions, right down to regulation house-slippers.

Instead of competing for stories or the boss's favor, people here engage in a philosophical one-upsmanship. Vegetarians who don't eat fish feel superior to those who do; vegetarians who don't eat fish and don't buy leather shoes feel "purer" yet. Feminists who don't shave their legs have a holier-than-thou attitude over those who simply don't wear makeup. There are several types of kibbutzim and there are even moral judgments made on what kind one chooses. Those people who choose to live on established kibbutzim—with paved sidewalks and mature trees—feel they must apologize to those who opt for a newly-created settlement without running water. "I really have the pioneer spirit, but I don't think it's fair to my children" is how the disclaimer usually starts. Never mind the fact that many people here have sold their homes and have left secure positions. They still feel that somehow they don't measure up—or down.

So when I return to my frenetic life, I'll remember that competition is a part of human nature and that even on a kibbutz, the most equitable of societies, equality is impossible.

Linda from Wales told me that economics had a lot to do with her decision to emigrate. "We were always worrying about making next month's rent," she said. "Here, I can be free of that."

She could not relate to some of the pressure that brought us here; I could not relate to the tension of her life. No one else's burdens seem quite as heavy as our own.

Dave and I had a really nice talk with Michael after school. We must have talked for an hour, telling him about some of the terrible things we did as kids. He was mesmerized. We've never done anything like that before. At home, as soon as we walked in the door, we were so desperately in need of decompression time that we parked him in front of the TV.

Yesterday we went to Jerusalem with Amir, who grew up

there. He took us to a seedy restaurant, where we dined on mixed grill. I didn't ask for the origin of the meat and he didn't volunteer. However, I did try to avoid the pieces that were still pulsating. Afterwards, we had coffee at a sidewalk cafe—in January. All those words—wind-chill factor, blizzard conditions, bronchial pneumonia—have been purged from my vocabulary. It feels so decadent.

January 25, 1985

Annoyances seem to roll off my back easier here. Whatever it is, I know it won't last forever because our stay is limited. Too bad I can't apply that same lesson to life in general.

February 5, 1985

Today we explored the caves at Bet Guvrin with Stanley and Rachaeli, our kibbutz "parents." The caves were eerily beautiful and one tunnel was so narrow we had to crawl along on our stomachs. It led to either an ancient mausoleum or a wine cellar, we weren't sure which.

The most peaceful part of the day was climbing to the top of a nearby mountain and drinking in the view. A blanket of desert flowers stretched out indefinitely. The air was so still, it was easy to feel that we were the last people on earth. I don't know when I've experienced such contentment. It was just one of those little slices of time that made our first month—indeed, our entire decision—seem very right.

All this serenity came to an abrupt end on our way home, when we had a flat tire near Hebron. Not only was the tire flat, but so was the spare. Stan told us not to worry because he was going to leave his gun and get help. While he was gone, we did the only thing we could do in a crisis: we ate lunch. Here we were, in the heart of Arab territory, sitting on the side of the road having a picnic.

February 10, 1985

Michael said "I hate you" to me for the first time. He has been uncooperative, but I think we're handling it better than we did at home.

Last night, for example, he had a dozen requests to stall bedtime—ranging from a Band-Aid for some mythical injury to complaints that his pillow was too hot and would I mind blowing on it? At the end of the work day, we were much quicker to lose our tempers. Here we can laugh at the transparency of it all.

Still, this reminds me that there are no panaceas. You can go to a place with no TV, no shopping malls, and no McDonald's and still have battles with your children. The real spadework doesn't go away just because the materialism does. A child still fights with another child whether it's over a Transformer or a stick. What transcends the geography is how you deal with it. Child-rearing is hard work, regardless of where you live. All we can do is give unlimited amounts of time, energy, and love—and that's still easier to do here than when the newspaper sucked everything out of me.

1

When the Office Is a Prison

Mark Ugowski, 30, is a very good architect with a very good firm. In fact, he was considered a bit of a *wunderkind*. He had worked on a number of glamorous projects and won several prestigious design awards, all before his 25th birthday. He had raced through his undergraduate years and architecture school at the University of Minnesota and now he was just where he wanted to be. Unfortunately, it wasn't enough.

"I told myself that I had a great job, prestige, financial security. At the time, I was engaged to a wonderful woman—but despite all of this, I felt empty. I thought of all the long hours, all the nights at the office, all the meetings. For so long, I had a compass to bring me to this exact spot and now that I had arrived, I wanted another compass."

A death in the family provided the catalyst he needed. A couple of years ago, his 21-year-old sister—who had no history of cardiac disease—suffered a fatal heart attack while walking across campus.

"It struck me how easily life can be snuffed out. One moment, you're doing something incredibly mundane and the next moment, it can all be over. After the funeral, we were going through

some of my sister's things and found these bills she had stashed
away. They didn't come to very much, but they obviously caused
her a great deal of anxiety. That's when it hit me how easy it is
for us to lose perspective. That whatever is a matter of life and
death—coming in under budget or getting a new client—really
isn't that way at all. It also made me realize that if there is
something you really want to do, do it now. Don't say 'I'll do it
when I'm 40' or 'when the mortgage is paid off' or 'after I'm vested
in the company,' because none of us have any guarantees.

"I needed time to sort out what I was doing with my life, so
I took a leave. When viewed in the context of an entire lifetime,
four months out of my career wasn't going to make that much
difference. I have some useful skills, some experience, a portfolio
that could get me back into architecture, if that is what I wanted.
But I had always had this dream of touching all four corners of
the United States and it was important enough to me that I was
willing to make some sacrifices. I knew that even without a regular
paycheck, I wouldn't starve. I couldn't swing fancy restaurants or
the theater, but I wasn't afraid to lower my standard of living."

Ugowski traveled for four months and indeed spent some
nights sleeping in his car. He would start his day eating a big
breakfast ("the cheapest meal and the most difficult to ruin") and
writing in his journal. He craved a life without limits, so the wide
open spaces of Montana and Wyoming and no itinerary suited him
just fine.

"Up until three days before my departure, I wasn't even going
to take a map. I rebelled against anything that smacked of boundaries or schedules. I didn't need a vacation; I needed to be totally
clear-headed and I couldn't have felt that way if I had to think
about the office."

He traveled from Minnesota to the Pacific Northwest, down
the California coast, and across the South. And then a funny thing
happened. "I remember it exactly—it was in Monticello, Virginia,
that I started thinking about efficient ways to use small spaces. By
the time I hit Boston, I was getting hot on architecture again. I
was itching to sit down at a drafting table, to use all these new
ideas and see if it made me a better designer."

To the casual observer, it may look as if Ugowski's sabbatical was in vain. He left—and returned—to architecture, but the experience cannot be so summarily dismissed. He is certain that the leave made him view his profession differently. "Before I left, I was more concerned with what other people thought. I worried about getting into an Ivy League school and being famous and getting my designs in magazines. Now, I'm more interested in whether a project is fun than whether it's prestigious. In fact, I discovered that it is the artistic side of the business that I really enjoy and the technical side that bogs me down. I would rather sell people on why they should buy our building than worry about where every nail goes, so I'm thinking about going into marketing. That was a revelation to me and one that I doubt I could have made while hunched over my work."

He also credits his leave with another discovery: that he really wanted to live in a warm climate. So, after never living more than a few hundred miles from his Milwaukee home, Ugowski moved to Palm Beach, Florida. "By traveling, I found out that there are good folks all over. If you're comfortable with yourself, you can be comfortable just about anywhere."

Palm trees are not a salve to every problem, and Ugowski is not so naive as to paint a picture of occupational bliss. "But when work starts getting too crazy, I catch myself. I'm sure clients liked me better before my leave, back when I was pouring every ounce of my heart and soul into a project. That's their job—to use as much of me as I allow. But keeping everything on an even keel, well, that's my job."

Arnie Zipursky, 30, shared some of the same traits and yearnings as Mark Ugowski. He was talented and ambitious enough to start his own film company, called Cambium Productions. People were constantly telling him and his wife, Fern, a social worker, that they had the world on a string. But, with a business to run, never did the world feel so out of reach.

The Toronto couple longed to travel, but business kept interfering with their plans, and as they looked ahead to the next decade, the situation would only get worse, not better. The couple wanted to buy a house and start a family, and unless they took their trip of a lifetime now, they were fearful that they would never get the chance. "I felt like I was caught in this impossible bind. I love what I do, but that doesn't mean I don't have other interests. I was worried that a few years from now, I'd resent the business because it robbed me of something I desperately wanted. It seemed as if there is the constant conflict of personal life versus career. Balancing the demands of one against the needs of the other."

Zipursky managed both by negotiating a nifty arrangement with his partner which gave them each four months off. "I figured if I longed for some adventure, he probably did, too. He didn't mind working hard to cover for my absence because he knew that his turn was coming up next. It worked because we both really trust each other."

Such cooperation enabled the Zipurskys to travel throughout the Far East, the Middle East, and Europe without worrying about who was minding the store. Right up to the time that they boarded the plane, there were big projects in the works—some that he had worked years to bring to fruition—but he never considered canceling the trip. To do so would be to subvert their goals to a bottom-line mentality—and it was precisely the distaste for such thinking that motivated him to carve out his own niche in the first place. "A lot of people go into business for themselves because they want to make their own decisions and take their own decisions and take their own risks and then they never do.

"I knew that other career opportunities would come along again, but I didn't know if I'd ever have another opportunity to see the world. Even though I was committed to the trip—and it was a goal that Fern and I had worked towards for a long time—I was still worried. I knew that there would be potential business losses; I just wanted to know that the losses would be offset by the gains of enriching our lives."

Any doubts evaporated as soon as they landed in Hong Kong. As for lost career opportunities, Zipursky returned to find one of Cambium's biggest plums just ready to fall from the tree: a contract with PBS for a weekly children's TV series, called "The Elephant Show."

Zipursky feels so strongly about the long-term benefits of a leave that he has initiated a program for his three employees. "I heard all the reasons why it simply could not be done, but the simple truth is that it can be done, providing you want it badly enough. I know that I returned a lot more alert and creative than when I left. Until you leave a job, you have no idea how caught up in it you really are."

Mark Ugowski and Arnie Zipursky saw a leave as a healthy response to a potentially unhealthy situation. They had the foresight to head stress off at the pass.

Unfortunately, most people don't think of a leave at a time when things are going relatively well. In fact, many don't even realize that they are significantly stressed until physical or psychological symptoms surface.

Stress has become a national epidemic. It used to be a response reserved for infrequent occasions—speaking to a large group, taking an exam, a trip to the dentist for a root canal. Today, it is our constant companion. Your blood pressure climbs abruptly as you idle in traffic, late for an important meeting, but powerless to do anything but watch the minutes on the digital clock flash away—a modern-day version of Chinese water torture. Your chest tightens as your boss tells you that the project you've poured every ounce of creativity into "needs something more." You go to the bank and the teller goes on break just as you get to the front of the line. At the supermarket, you unload a cartful of groceries, only to find out that they won't accept a personal check. It goes on and on—all the while, pupils dilate, stomach muscles tense, eyes twitch, and breathing becomes rapid.

It is ironic that having eradicated many of the diseases of the past—tuberculosis, polio, and scarlet fever—we are now falling victim to a disease of choice. Whether you call it burnout, mid-life crisis, the blahs, or the blues, it is exacting a high toll from the American work place.

Just looking at the numbers is enough to make your palms sweat:

  • Some 42 million Americans have hypertension. A study conducted by the University of North Carolina revealed that stress appears to reduce the kidneys' ability to remove excess sodium, thus contributing to hypertension.

- More than 70 million tranquilizer prescriptions are issued each year. Valium is the leading brand-name drug prescribed in the United States today, followed closely by Inderal (for high blood pressure) and Tagamet (for ulcers).
- The National Council on Compensation Insurance (NCCI) revealed that cumulative mental-stress claims accounted for 11 percent of all occupational disease claims filed last year. "The rapid increase in stress-related claims is threatening to bankrupt workers' compensation programs," said Dr. Paul Rosch, director of the American Institute of Stress in Yonkers, New York.
- Cocaine is the preferred drug of 5 million Americans. One study indicated that the United States loses about 1,000 students (the equivalent of seven medical-school graduating classes) each year to drug addiction, alcoholism, and suicide.
- An alarming increase in the incidence of stomach disorders, such as colitis, ileitis, and ulcers have occurred since 1970. Women—staking their claim in the business world—have now staked a claim in ulcer territory as well. Twenty years ago, males with ulcers outnumbered females 20 to 1; today that figure is 2 to 1.

However, what has really caused corporate America to sit up and take notice is that stress is expensive. According to Rosch, it costs the country $150 billion annually—or about $1,500 for every U.S. worker—in absenteeism, lost productivity, and direct medical costs.

The human costs are more difficult to measure. Who can put a price tag on broken marriages, lapsed friendships, little or no relationship with one's children?

What makes stress so alarming is its pervasiveness. When we talk about someone who needs two martinis just to unclench his jaws at night, we can no longer assume it is the hard-charging mogul overseeing an international empire or the commodities broker trading millions by the minute.

Today, it can just as easily be the salesperson whose commissions have fallen off and is now taking some heat from the home office, the executive recruiter whose life is a blur of airports and

Holiday Inns, or the teacher who is harangued by the school board to modify the curriculum. It can be any parent who is asked to stay late at the office and is furiously trying to finish before the day-care center closes at six.

Dr. Gale Levin, a Connecticut psychiatrist and a mother of two children, both aged under eighteen months, notes: "Stress is not listed in any medical books as a specific psychiatric disorder, but we see it every day. In fact, most of the people I know have it."

In its most extreme forms, the results are alcohol and drug abuse, cardiac arrest, or suicide. More commonly, it surfaces in any number of physical ailments, from headaches to hypertension (see following list of symptoms). The ones that show up on the EKG or stomach X-ray are easy to pinpoint, but there is no blood test or X-ray that can detect the damage that stress can do to one's soul. It is, however, crucial to pick up this damage early before it causes a type of motivational paralysis.

The factors that trigger stress, called "stressors," can build up until one is engulfed by a sense of helplessness. This is why, despite intense unhappiness, some people are unable to move off square one—to leave the job, marriage, or whatever it is that is causing so much pain. They put themselves in constant conflict, wanting out, but ready with all kinds of excuses why they can't head for the exits: they're making too much money, they have too much seniority, or there are bad bosses all over. They perceive themselves as having no options and are therefore powerless to act— even in their own best interests. If and when they finally do, it's usually impulsively. Rather than thoughtful action, it's desperate reaction.

PHYSIOLOGICAL SYMPTOMS
OF STRESS

Cardiovascular symptoms
Heart pounding
Heart racing or beating erratically

Cold, sweaty hands
Headaches (throbbing pain)

Respiratory symptoms

Rapid, erratic, or shallow breathing
Shortness of breath
Asthma attack
Difficulty in speaking because of poor breathing control

Muscular symptoms

Headaches (steady pain)
Back or shoulder pains
Muscle tremors or hands shaking
Arthritis
Trembling

Gastrointestinal symptoms

Upset stomach, nausea, or vomiting
Constipation
Diarrhea
Sharp abdominal pains
Stomach churning
Strong and frequent need to defecate

Skin symptoms

Acne
Dandruff
Perspiration
Excessive dryness of skin or hair
Flushing

Immunity symptoms

Allergy flare-up
Catching colds
Catching the flu
Skin rash

Metabolic symptoms

Increased appetite

Increased craving for tobacco or sweets
Thoughts racing or difficulty sleeping
Feelings of crawling anxiety or nervousness
Listlessness

PSYCHOLOGICAL AND
BEHAVIORAL SYMPTOMS OF STRESS

Excessive worrying
Short fuse
Irritability
Crying for little or no reason
Feeling depressed
Uncontrollable anger
Fatigue
Frustration
Anxiety
Sleep difficulties
Decreased performance level

Nella Barkley, a counselor at the John C. Crystal Job Center in New York, saw the consequences first-hand when a friend who had spent twenty-three years in publishing abruptly quit.

"One day, she walked into her boss's office and submitted her resignation," Barkley said. "Her reasons were that she had been married to her organization and needed to put some distance between herself and her work. This woman was absolutely superior at her job. It's a pity that she had to resort to such drastic measures to get some personal time. And this is not an isolated case. If only we could get hold of these people five or ten years earlier, we could help them restructure the work place to meet *their* needs. It's like detecting small tremors before they become major earthquakes."

The problem, however, is that many people ignore the tremors or consider them too trivial to do anything about. Boredom, cynicism, chronic fatigue, feeling overwhelmed, dreading Monday mornings, all are easily brushed off as "insignificant," but are the warning signals that today's burnout victims failed to heed five years ago.

"Of course, everyone has these feelings from time to time," said Levin. "But, for example, when occasional moodiness turns into constant irritability, it's a sign that the circuits are getting overloaded. A couple of weeks isn't very long, but six months or longer would indicate some kind of change is in order. Don't wait until your sanity is on the line to take action. Take control now."

The antidote to stress is control, a commodity that is in very short supply. It is evident in the way people describe their jobs. Several leave-takers described themselves as "a twig being carried along in the current" or described their world as "spinning out of orbit." It is not uncommon to hear people describe their work-loads as disasters: as being buried, drowning, or suffocating in work. It is the employee as victim.

The real tragedy, according to Brian Gould, a San Francisco psychologist, is that it wasn't always that way. Without exception, most employees who are casualties of job-related stress were at one time extremely talented and capable people. Said Gould: "It is the affliction of people who start out as outstanding employees. Before you burn out, there was a time when you had to be on fire."

WHO IS MOST VULNERABLE?

The stereotype of the stressed-out employee is the "type A" personality—the term coined by cardiologist Meyer Friedman in 1974, which became national slang for the harried, hostile, achievement-obsessed executive, who barks and bellows his way through the day. But since many cool personalities on the surface are really seething underneath, there are many doctors who feel you can't make assumptions about a person's anxiety level just because he never raises his voice.

More often, it is the environment rather than the personality that leads to burnout. "A state of fatigue or frustration brought about by devotion to a cause, way of life or relationship that failed to produce the expected reward" is the definition offered by psychotherapist Herbert J. Freudenberger in his book *Burnout.*

It isn't working as much as it is being thwarted. That explains why a fulfilled employee can work twice the hours—even erratic ones—as a frustrated employee can and not feel nearly as tired.

Experts put those at risk in four groups:

1) Where there is a minimum of opportunity for personal rewards and satisfaction.

Note that the key phrase is "personal rewards," not financial ones. Dentists are well compensated for their work, yet, as a profession, have one of the highest rates of burnout. They graduate in their early 20s, they are in a highly technical field, and they make a lot of money. Said Gould: "By the time they are in their early 40s, they are operating at their technical peak. There isn't a lot of challenge, their ambitions have been fulfilled, so they lose interest and stop practicing dentistry."

Gould also cited some areas of law—particularly domestic relations—as paying few emotional dividends. "You have superb practitioners facing extremely stressful situations, such as divorce and custody cases. This is where what is legally good can be humanly bad. Dedicated lawyers could have done a fine job with everyone being miserable. Where is the satisfaction?"

2) When you have difficulty distancing yourself from your job.

The social worker who gets overly involved in his cases, the clergyman who is on twenty-four-hour call, the nurse who deals with terminally ill patients, are just a few examples of people in professions with high susceptability to burnout. And those with jobs that require distance and objectivity—such as journalists—have a difficult time dropping the professional persona in order to be intimate and nurturing with their families.

3) Where there's little "down" time.

This used to be limited to air-traffic controllers, but today it could be any employee who is working under unreasonable time constraints, from an assembly-line worker to a middle manager trying to crank out the same amount of work with fewer people.

Increased competition, a volatile economy, and constantly changing technology have put just about everyone in the hot seat. And
it doesn't stop at 6 P.M. For families juggling dual careers, it means
getting off work and going to work: dinner, homework, laundry,
bedtime. On the weekend, there are social and family obligations.
The only "down" time comes when you climb into bed at night—
and by that time you and your spouse are too tired to do anything
but fall asleep watching the ten o'clock news.

4) People with little or no control in their positions.
Employees who have all the responsibility and none of the
authority—usually middle managers—are prime burnout candidates, according to a study at Washington University in St. Louis.
A study of 300 middle managers in a variety of industries cast
doubt on the stereotype of the harried top executive. "They have
the ability to make things happen; but it is the employees who have
limited authority and are not properly rewarded who are the most
at risk," the study reported.

Authority was enough to make Linda Anderson, a Washington, D.C. nursing supervisor, switch from days to nights. "During
the day, there are so many doctors and administrators around.
Sometimes you have to answer to more than one boss and it's very
easy to get caught in the middle of a power struggle. You don't
know *who* you're supposed to please. At night, you don't have so
many people second-guessing you. I'm able to care for patients—
which is the reason why I got into nursing—instead of getting
caught up in a lot of game-playing."

Anderson made her decision to swap her 8-to-4, five-days-a-
week schedule for the graveyard shift after she took a summer off
to spend with her two grade-school children.

Anderson put her leave to excellent use—for reassessment of
work and the position it held in her life. A leave should not be
regarded as a panacea for stress or the answer to a dreadful job.
If it is just a temporary relief, it could be no different than taking
a drink or popping a tranquilizer—only more expensive.

Said Gould: "A lot of people take time off when what they
really need is a job change. A sabbatical is not going to alter your

feeling if you're returning to a situation you hate. It's like taking a pot off a burner and then putting it back on. It will take longer, but it will still boil over."

OTHER WAYS OF COPING

It was always the office equipment, never the people, that got the tune-up. All that is changing, as more companies are meeting burnout head-on. A few years ago, to admit to "battle fatigue" would be unspeakable; today, stress-management seminars are all the rage. However, there are some companies that have gone even further. At H.A. Montgomery, a small chemical manufacturer in Detroit, sick days have dropped 72 percent since the company began paying for any employee who wanted to learn transcendental meditation. At Tenneco, Inc., an oil conglomerate in Houston, employees can unwind in the Jacuzzi, sauna, or anywhere else in the company's $11 million health club. However, for sheer ingenuity, credit must go to Panasonic, where employees can practice primal scream therapy in a soundproof, padded room.

Anxiety is not something that can be turned on and off like a garden hose and, certainly, breaking into a mantra is not going to be a very satisfying solution for someone who wants to be snorkeling in the Virgin Islands. The following suggestions, culled from health experts, are not intended to take the place of time out. But they can help you cope while you're plotting your escape:

Exercise. People who have no way of discharging stress in a recreational way are prime candidates for burnout. Exercise is very important, especially for office workers and anyone else who sits all day. (You have to do *something* with all that bottled-up adrenaline.) But watch out for turning exercise into just another goal. Jogging doesn't necessarily mean that you have to become a marathoner. The objective is relaxation, not achievement.

Good nutrition. You've heard it all before. Keep your weight down, lower your cholesterol, eat more high-fiber foods, and shake the salt habit. Fast-trackers are notorious for living on cigarettes and vending-machine coffee, and grabbing a danish, blowing their hair, and watching "The Today Show"—all at the same time. Leave yourself enough time for three real meals a day.

Manage your time; don't let time manage you. Along with relaxation exercises, most stress-management programs include time-management techniques, which zero in on establishing priorities. What do you have to do, what do you want to do, and what do you neither want to nor have to do? (For example, lawn work could be eliminated as a weekend burden by hiring someone to do it for you.) If you had only six months to live, how many of these items would be a concern?

Shaking out the minutiae from your life will result in extra leisure time. Be extra vigilant about protecting it. Don't let work slosh over into what is rightfully yours. Are you carrying work home out of habit rather than necessity? Are you staying late because you're spinning your wheels during normal working hours? (After coffee breaks, lunch, and "networking," is it 3 P.M. before you actually start tackling that "in" box?) Some employees stay way beyond quitting time because they see others doing the same thing and they're afraid that they won't look as committed as their co-workers. Others just assume that it will earn them some extra points with the boss. A newspaper colleague, one of the most dedicated journalists I've ever met, routinely put in sixty-hour weeks for five years—and never heard a word from management. One day, she said, "Enough is enough," and stopped. She came in at 9 and left at 5 and never showed her face on the weekends. Her superiors' reaction? None. Her conclusion was that all that extra effort had been neither recognized nor appreciated.

"No one has to work late on a regular basis," said Linda Rawlings, one of two therapists who has counseled nearly 900 employees at the *Los Angeles Times.* "And no one needs to eat lunch at his or her desk. I'm not talking about the occasional time when a special project is due. I'm talking about when this kind of behavior becomes the norm. Either you're not managing your time correctly or there is a problem with the job itself."

Expand your horizons. Sheldon Zipursky, a Toronto psychiatrist, kept burnout at bay by investing in his brother's film production company. ("I got to read scripts and meet more interesting people than doctors.") Mary Veeder, who teaches freshman English at Indiana University, enriches her life by writing movie reviews for a local newspaper. Craig Rasmussen, in sales for Xerox, picks up extra bucks and strokes for the ego by modeling. If you put all your eggs in one basket, then what do you do when the basket breaks? Time and again, therapists stressed that the people who cope best are the ones who have interests outside of work.

Take on-the-job breaks. Don't stay at your desk all day. Get up and walk around the building or around the block. Shift into an activity completely different from work. If you have to use your eyes on detailed paperwork or staring at a computer screen, listen to music. If you have to deal with the public all day, then go somewhere quiet and read.

Avoid chemicals. One definition of stress is the loss of control; chemicals give the perception of being in control, which explains why alcohol and drug use is alarmingly high in the work force. Shun drugs and tobacco, drink alcohol only in moderation, and take steps to limit your caffeine consumption. They all can trigger mood fluctuations.

Learn relaxation techniques. Try some mental exercises to create a sense of tranquility—even where none exists. It doesn't have to be anything elaborate: Just sitting in a quiet room and breathing deeply from the diaphragm can loosen the "knots" of tension. (Deep breathing requires only twelve breaths a minute, compared to the eighteen shallow breaths a minute we normally take.) An exercise that is sometimes used in conjunction with deep breathing involves concentration on relaxing successive sets of muscles from the tips of your toes to the muscles in your forehead and neck.

Another particularly effective technique is called imagery, best used when your mind is racing ahead and you want to shut it off and get some rest. Visualize a very peaceful scene, perhaps somewhere you have visited on vacation (if you have a photo to keep on your desk as a visual cue, even better), or a childhood memory such as walking hand in hand with your father to get ice cream. Let the sense of calm literally push out the anxiety. If you are facing a big project, it also helps to visualize the completed task. This worked for Mary Lou Retton, who pictured herself performing her gymnastic routines perfectly at the 1984 Olympics. If she could "see" herself getting "10s" from the judges, then you can see yourself handing in a nice fat report to your boss by Monday morning.

Practice self-talk. We talk to ourselves in ways that would be appalling if they came from someone else. Instead of flagellating yourself for losing your keys or missing a meeting ("You stupid idiot! I can't believe you did that!") try a more positive message ("O.K. You screwed up. You've done it before and you'll do it again, but that doesn't mean that the world is coming to an end").

Get counseling. There are times when just unloading to your friends isn't enough.
Professional help from a psychologist, social worker, or therapist can head you in the right direction. Don't be afraid to ask for that help.

Take charge. Ultimately, you are responsible for your own happiness, not your employer or your family. Change what you can (if waiting in line is torture, than don't shop during peak hours). Accept what you can't (you loathe your brother in law, but you love your sister more).
Paul Camic, co-director of the Behavioral Medicine and Health Promotion Program at the University of Chicago Medical Center, conducts stress-reduction programs for the "executive family." He divided patients into three categories: "the ones who genuinely want to change, the ones who say they want to reduce stress but aren't willing to put forth the effort, and the ones who really don't want to because they get more attention for complaining than they will for being healthy."

DECIDING TO TAKE A TIME OUT

Stress triggers a fight-or-flight response. When a person feels great anxiety, hormones are released into the bloodstream, senses sharpen, breathing and heart rate increase, blood pressure climbs, and muscles tense—all okay if you're a caveman facing a tyrannosaurus but inappropriate for someone being called in by the boss for a job evaluation.

So having tried the fight, that leaves only flight. This may certainly be the most appropriate response for someone who is in healthy physical and mental condition and just feels a nagging sense of dissatisfaction that life isn't as pleasurable as it could be. (Think about it. When was the last time you heard anyone say, "You know, I'm just having *too* much fun."?) Then you open a memo reprimanding you for not getting your expenses in by the first of the month, or you knock yourself out on a project and nobody even said "thanks," and suddenly you think, "These guys don't deserve my best years, my best energy, my best everything. What am I doing here?"

"There is an inordinate respect for the work ethic in this country," said psychiatrist Levin. "People want to do their best, but they get the message that they're not accomplishing anything and they're not appreciated. It is not an indictment of workers as much as the work place."

WHY NOT A LONG VACATION?

A vacation is certainly one way to combat stress. But, for most people, two weeks lounging around the pool sipping banana daiquiris can't relieve twelve months of accumulated stress. Dr. Jerome Bergheim, a Miami psychiatrist, said that it usually takes one week for the average person just to unwind from their work environment. (And if you have the kind of job that requires you to "work ahead" to compensate for your absence, then it can take even longer.) All rather depressing news, when you consider that the average American vacation lasts a mere 5.8 days. So even if

you have a month off, close to half of your time has slipped away
before you can start capitalizing on the benefits. This in turn
produces an inherent pressure to squeeze in as much as you can
before you return. It's the "blood bank theory" of leisure time: If
I see and do everything and store up on good times while I'm on
vacation, then I can draw on these memories later when I'm back
at work. Unfortunately, it doesn't work that way. The frenetic
activity only creates more tension, any memories are blurred
rather than savored, and, consequently, all you're left with is a
case of exhaustion.

I am someone whose job requires that a reasonable amount of
creativity be expended daily; so I likened my mind to a gas tank.
When I came home at night, the needle was on "empty." The next
morning, it would have nudged up a little; after a particularly
restful weekend, it might go all the way up to a quarter-tank and
after a really terrific vacation, it might get up to the halfway point.
But it never got to full.

There is no denying that the person who takes time out, who
now has time on his side, sees with different eyes than someone
who is just "passing through." You notice colors, textures, con-
tours, and nuances of speech and behavior in a way that could
never be possible on a "If-it's-Tuesday-this-must-be-Belgium"
trip. Paul Theroux said there's a difference between being a traveler and being a tourist. "Tourists want to go on vacation to rest
and be taken care of; travelers want to discover."

Discovery, participation, experience—these are the souvenirs
that leave-takers have when they return. When they come home,
it is with more than sand in the swimsuit, but with a sense of calm.

Of course, you don't need to go to the other side of the world
to regain equilibrium.

Susan Reidel, an employee of Wells Fargo, fulfilled her fantasy
to be a writer by moving out of the fast lane for three months and
working on a children's book. "It would have been impossible for
me to achieve that during a vacation. The last time I had something published was when I was 17," said Reidel, who is now 38.
"I wanted to work back into a routine, to immerse myself in good
writing, so there were days on vacation when all I did was read.

Just at the time I was ready to write myself, I would have gone back to work. I would have gone back to my demanding schedule and it would have just died right there. But it didn't. This leave gave me momentum."

HOW MUCH AND WHAT FOR?

Deciding how much time you need is a highly individual decision, which can be determined by finances, employer's needs, and the activity itself. Three months is a good chunk of time if you're going to lay in the backyard hammock, but for die-hard sailors, it is barely enough time to get their feet wet.

The first step is to determine just how you want to spend your time. Zeroing in on what you want and like to do will give your dreams shape and scope. If you want to study harmony and counterpoint at the Juilliard School of Music, you know exactly how long the course will last and what it will cost; and if you're going to apply for a scholarship, it will impose a timetable. Studying the piano at home, however, is a much more open-ended endeavor.

If you have no specific avocation, but are interested in everything, winnow down your choices. Not only is a specific purpose easier to sell to your employer, but it makes your leave more manageable. Right now, you may think you want nothing more than to become a couch potato and watch "I Dream of Jeannie" reruns, but combining your time at home with, say, a course in film criticism will make it easier to convince your boss. Bear in mind too that another leave will probably not come your way for quite a while. Accomplishing something tangible on your sabbatical will allow you to return to work with a feeling of satisfaction. On the other hand, returning with nothing to show for it may only add to your feelings of frustration.

To help you discover what it is you'd like to do with your time out, try putting down on paper some of your all-time great life experiences. What is it that really gives you a kick? A newspaper colleague, who greatly enjoyed teaching his own kids to read, for example, used time away to initiate a local literacy program. A doctor who never forgot the roar of the greasepaint from his college theater days, worked three months in summer stock. Perhaps the most creative sabbatical-taker has been Dr. John Coleman, the former president of Haverford College. During his first four-month leave in 1972, he left academia to work as a garbage collector in Philadelphia (though sanitation probably wasn't on *his* list of great life experiences). Eleven years later, he took another four months and joined the legions of homeless on the streets of New York. On his last sabbatical, in 1986, he worked as an apprentice to a chef. The experience was the catalyst in purchasing an inn, in Chester, Vermont.

For many, the peak memories come from travel. People who cannot remember what they had for breakfast can recall a visit to the Acropolis two decades earlier with perfect clarity. There are leave-takers who concentrate on one country to explore their ethnic roots or return to a spot they sampled all too hastily on a charter blitz.

Even if you aren't intrigued by one particular country, your "peak experiences" list may reveal an answer. Learning tennis? (A tennis camp for the winter season.) Accolades for a gourmet meal? (A stint at the American Culinary Institute, training ground for some of the country's best chefs.) Hearing Isaac Stern at Carnegie Hall? (Violin lessons.) Renovating your "handyman's special"? (A tour with Partnership for Productivity International, which puts carpentry skills to good use in Third-World countries.)

If you're traveling with another person or as a family, make sure that everyone's interests are represented. (One couple drew up separate lists and then based their itinerary on the countries that were chosen by both.) Regardless of your methodology, a frank discussion on not only the where but the why is in order. (This topic is discussed further in the next chapter.)

Deciding between structured or unstructured time doesn't need to be an either-or situation. For example, we took the best of both by spending six months on a kibbutz, where there was a daily regimen, followed by two months of spontaneity traveling through Europe.

Above all, be attuned to your needs. If you are in a job that demands precision, you may need a stint at a potter's wheel. If you are bored by work, you could benefit by a program like Outward Bound, which teaches wilderness survival.

Some people of course just hang out.

Andy Thomas, 32, asked for an unpaid leave after her husband died of a heart attack. For nine years, she had taught special education, but then she had a disagreement with a parent and felt betrayed when the school administration would not back her up. "Coming on the heels of my husband's death, I just didn't have the emotional reserves," she said.

How did Thomas spend her year? She traveled, she completed some long-overdue craft projects, she saw friends without canceling five times before she could fit them into her schedule. To support her hiatus, she worked at a boutique. "It was very finite. You rang up the cash register and the transaction was over; but teaching—particularly with special-need kids—is an ongoing process. I would never want to do it (sales) for a living, but it felt great to summon up that energy that I would normally put into my job and put it into myself."

Thomas returned to the classroom in September 1986. What will she remember most from her time out? "The biggest pleasure was that I could take my time getting ready in the morning. There was nowhere I *had* to be. I went in feeling bewildered and came out knowing that I could tolerate loneliness . . . that I could rely on myself for my own fulfillment."

Stress Index

The University of New Hampshire 1984 study, ranking states by their "stress index," starting with the most stressful states as determined by 15 statistical indicators.

1/Nevada	26/North Carolina
2/Alaska	27/Texas
3/Georgia	28/New Mexico
4/Washington	29/Arkansas
5/Oregon	30/Pennsylvania
6/Alabama	31/West Virginia
7/California	32/Missouri
8/Mississippi	33/Kansas
9/Arizona	34/Hawaii
10/Tennessee	35/Indiana
11/Colorado	36/Rhode Island
12/Oklahoma	37/Connecticut
13/South Carolina	38/Maine
14/Florida	39/Wyoming
15/Michigan	40/Vermont
16/New York	41/Massachusetts
17/Illinois	42/Montana
18/Idaho	43/Minnesota
19/Virginia	44/Utah
20/Kentucky	45/New Hampshire
21/Ohio	46/Wisconsin
22/Louisiana	47/North Dakota
23/Delaware	48/South Dakota
24/Maryland	49/Iowa
25/New Jersey	50/Nebraska

Figures used apply to residents of the states, not tourists. Calculations based on 1978 statistics for 15 stress-related indicators; this was the last year for which data from all states was available when the study began four years ago. *Source: Social Stress in the United States* (Dover, Mass.: Auburn House, 1986).

February 14, 1985

Valentine's Day passed unnoticed here, which is why I probably felt homesick for Western civilization. We went into Jerusalem, found a restaurant that served real hamburgers, and saw our first movie. It should have been something like The Ten Commandments *or* Exodus. *Instead, it was* The Karate Kid. *Subtitles in French, Spanish, Russian, and Hebrew took up half the screen, but it was still great fun. At home, this would have been a weekly occurrence; here it became a special occasion. That's just the kind of scaling down that I hoped to accomplish.*

Had a nice talk with a kibbutznik in the factory. She likes this lifestyle because of the equality and because everyone is held in the same esteem, whether they scrub floors, teach children, or harvest fields. "The trouble with Americans is that you think you are what you do. That's not a perception shared by the rest of the world," she said. Maybe that's why there are so many doctors here driving tractors.

February 20, 1985

We took a "field trip" to Jericho. However, the most indelible sight wasn't the ruins but the haunting faces of a Bedouin family that came running up to the bus, begging for money. The poverty here is difficult for any American to comprehend. It was a good lesson for Michael, whose definition of poor was any kid without a dirt bike. It's one thing to tell children about poverty and quite another to let them see it first-hand.

The highlight of the day was planting trees on this fledgling settlement on the West Bank. We looked out on this limitless horizon—with nothing but the Jordanian mountains staring back. To swing a hoe into this parched earth and pat dirt around a scruffy twig was something I never could have experienced from behind my desk. At the planting, I met a woman, exactly my age, whose grandparents came from the same Polish shtetl as mine. The only difference was that her family emigrated to Israel, while mine passed through Ellis Island. How ironic that we started out in the same part of the world, took vastly different routes, and ended up in exactly the same place.

2

Making the Break

The lives of most mid-career professionals have about as much spontaneity as triple-bypass surgery—and are about as much fun.

You have responsibilities—lots of them. You may have a spouse and children and parents. You have bills that arrive on the first of the month whether you're there or not. And you save everything from canceled checks to Beluga whales. This is not an existence that can easily be stuffed into a duffel bag and thrown over a shoulder.

"Sure, I'd love to put my life on hold and escape to Tahiti," said one commodities broker. "Just tell me how to put my mortgage, my car payment, my Master Card bill, and my alimony on hold as well."

The fantasy of bolting from your office, whipping off your tie, jumping into a Porsche, and roaring down the highway, leaving civilization far behind is the stuff that scripts are made of. You won't be able to make your getaway with such abandon—after all, this is real life—but your getaway *can* be accomplished.

Over the years, you make a lot of sacrifices for your career. Just keep in mind that your leave is one of the rewards. Not everyone will share that view, but it is crucial that there be at least some consensus among the people whose lives will be directly affected.

SUPPOSE YOUR SPOUSE
WON'T GO?

When Mary Ocwieja married Bill Smith the two family-practice physicians exchanged the traditional vows along with a more unusual one—that Ocwieja would spend four months in Thailand.

Before she was married, Ocwieja lived and worked in Thailand as part of her residency training. While her salary was small, the real payoff came from the gratitude of her patients and the knowledge that she was bringing quality medical care to people who would otherwise not have access to it. "Every day, I could see the impact of my work," she said. "I really felt like I was making a contribution. It got in my blood and I knew that I would have to get back."

Her husband makes a contribution to people, too, but in a small office in Rice Lake, Wisconsin, where he does everything from delivering babies to geriatrics. The chance of Smith leaving his practice for four months is nil. When asked how they resolved the issue, Smith shrugged his shoulders. "I understand her need to go and she can understand my need to be here with my patients."

Career-oriented couples grapple with work-related issues every day—from who is going to run home at lunch to meet the TV repairman to who can stand in line at the post office for an hour during the holiday rush to who is going to stay home with a sick child. These are the not so small quandaries of day-to-day living, decided on the basis of who is most efficient, most capable, most available. But, sometimes, the issues are on a larger scale, such as when your spouse gets a fantastic job offer on the other side of the country and you already have an equally fantastic job on the other side of town.

Taking a leave involves many of the same decisions necessary in a job relocation, without the long-term ramifications. In a perfect world, both people arrive at the same decision at the same time, but, in reality, it is the rare couple who hit the peaks and valleys of work simultaneously. You come home clutching an article on Caribbean cruising and he takes the wind out of your sails by saying he was just promoted and is now in for a year of sixty-hour workweeks.

Why is life never simple?

"Marriage, like life, is constantly changing," said Harvey Ruben, a New Haven, Connecticut, psychiatrist. "Because of this, marital passages—periods of severe and relationship-threatening stress—are inevitable. Each one gives us the opportunity to help each other. In doing so, we grow stronger in our relationship and more sure of ourselves; as we come through each passage, our marriage grows and thrives."

Well, some marriages do. With a national divorce rate that hovers around fifty percent, it is painfully clear that change can upset the ever-delicate balance between couples. But why is it that one couple can maneuver around obstacles with all the deftness of slalom skiiers, while for others, the tiniest bump sends them sprawling? One day you can hear a story about a couple who relocated and how it blossomed into a time of personal growth that brought them closer together. The next day you can hear that the very same set of circumstances affected another couple completely differently, engendering feelings of resentment that eventually led to a divorce.

Psychiatrists point to the fact that such problems are symptomatic of other unresolved issues that have been swept under the rug—sometimes for years. Any disruption to the status quo—whether it's an impending move, a baby, or a job change—brings these issues to the surface, where they can no longer be ignored.

What is finally resolved is not nearly as important as *how* it is resolved. It doesn't really matter what decision a couple makes, as long as it was predicated on love, respect, equality, trust, and, above all, communication.

"For any couple to cope with predictable crises means that there needs to be an ongoing dialogue," said Ruben. "Presumably they've been dealing with career issues all along, so they have had some experience with 'my priorities versus your priorities.'

They've already had to deal with job offers, out-of-town travel, working on weekends, and cutting a vacation short because of an emergency at the office. If it's a well-functioning marriage, they will be able to discuss the issue rationally and wisely and find some common ground. If it's not, any negotiations will break down because each will want to pursue his or her own ends."

Ruben favors the word "negotiations" over "compromise." "The problem with compromise is that it's giving in. We may feel noble, but we don't feel satisfied. But negotiation means that you look at my way and I look at your way and then we come up with something that becomes our way. It demands the best and most creative efforts of each."

Sometimes, those best efforts yield a solution that doesn't look satisfactory at all—taking a leave alone.

In the twenty-five couples I interviewed on the subject, virtually every one would have preferred to go with their spouses. But the realities of jobs and children and economics intruded, making other arrangements necessary. The ones who did go it alone did so only after weighing the costs and benefits, of deciding what was best for "our careers," "our children," and "our mental health," until they came up with a solution that made sense in the context of their lives.

That was certainly the case for Joel Havemann, projects editor at the *Washington Times,* and his wife, Judy Nichol, national editor at the *Washington Post.* In 1979, Nichol won a Neiman Fellowship to Harvard. At the time, Havemann was employed by the *National Journal,* a small but prestigious magazine.

"They just couldn't let people go, the way a big place like the *Post* could," Havemann said. "It would have been a shame for Judy to miss such an opportunity. I never considered asking her to give it up on my account, any more than she would have asked me to give up my job. So I commuted up to Boston as many weekends as I could. Our marriage is very strong and we knew that we could survive the separation."

When Susan Feyder Peterson, a business reporter in Minneapolis, was one of nine Bagheot Fellows chosen for a year at Columbia University, the decision to leave her husband, David Peterson, behind was purely an economic one. "We just could not afford to lose half of our income. There was never any question that David would stay, but that doesn't mean it was easy. I greatly underestimated just how tough it would be," said Feyder, who saw her husband three times in nine months. Her husband agreed that it was a difficult period, but one that yielded some marital, as well as career, benefits. Said Peterson, "I certainly appreciate Susan more than I did before and I certainly don't take our relationship for granted."

What made it so tough? "First, I was back in school after a thirteen-year absence; second, I was going from a house to a dinky apartment; and third, I had a great deal of anxiety about succeeding. I'm glad I did it, but I would never do it again. Maybe I would feel differently if I had done something pleasurable."

Lois Foley, a Dallas public relations executive, did exactly that, taking three months off to see the Orient with her best friend from high school. Her husband, Steve Foley, sells pharmaceuticals and had no interest in traipsing around China. "Lois and I have completely different definitions of leisure time," he said. "I like to go somewhere where I'm going to be pampered—room service, Broadway shows, nice dinners—and she likes to put on a pair of khaki shorts and a T-shirt and camp out."

Foley admits to lobbying for her husband to join her, but after weighing the pros and cons she abandoned the campaign. "This shouldn't be the sort of thing that you have to talk someone into. If he had consented to please me, I would have felt this pressure to make sure he was having a good time. He would have been miserable, wishing he was at home; I would have been miserable because I had this once-in-a-lifetime opportunity that may never come around again and it wasn't what I had planned. Neither of us would have gotten what we wanted; this way, we both did."

Just how willing one mate is to accommodate the other is a reflection of the health of the marriage, according to Dr. Gale Levin. In the case of the Foleys, the real issue wasn't the Orient, it was control.

"Even in the calmest of times, there are all sorts of issues that couples end up arguing about. Some of them are downright silly—what movie to see, for example, whether to sleep with the window open or closed, who takes out the garbage—but the real question is 'Who has more power?' "

Therapists recognize that behind every argument about garbage or money or children lurk the more volatile matters of autonomy, power, and self-esteem. Of who is doing the dominating and who is doing the deferring.

Couples can break out of their power struggles by keeping the lines of communication open and searching for ways to take a step towards the middle. For example, Joel Havemann couldn't join his wife at Harvard, but he could visit one weekend out of every month.

Some couples—who can get along without one income but not two—have found satisfaction in taking turns. ("You take three months to write your novel, then I'll take three months to write my screenplay.") It's the mid-life version of "You put me through graduate school, now I'll put you through graduate school."

"It's the desire—the sincere effort of two people to reach some middle ground—that is crucial," Levin said. "That takes two emotionally stable people who are as concerned about the other person as they are about themselves. If a spouse automatically rejects the idea of a leave out of hand, it just makes the situation worse. On the surface, it appears as if nothing has changed—indeed, she is going off to her office this morning, like she did yesterday morning and the morning before that—but the climate has changed because he rejected the idea automatically. Instead, he could have tried to find some part of the request to agree with—say, 'I can't take a year, but I can take a summer' or 'This quarter looks bad, but if you wait till next quarter, I'm sure I can work out something.' Everyone appreciates a good-faith effort, and coming up with some alternative to put on the table will keep the communication—and perhaps your marriage—from deteriorating."

Experts offer the following guidelines for resolving conflicts. It may not make your mate see your point of view, but it will keep discussions from escalating into full-scale battles:

• Never try to deal with major problems when you're angry. If the time isn't right, set up a specific time to have a serious talk with your spouse about your need for time out.

- Never resort to name-calling. Instead of labeling your spouse as "selfish" because he refuses to see your point of view, zero in on your feelings. Talk about what it would mean to you to have a well-defined period of time away—or what it means to you to have a financial cushion.

- Avoid dictating a course of action. If you state "This is what I need and here's one solution" rather than "This is what I need and here's what I think we should do," it makes the other partner far less defensive.

- When constructing a reciprocal agreement, be specific. It is not enough to say "If I can take the summer off to take a photography course, you can have the winter off to ski." Where? When? For how long? Will one person have to invest in a lot of new equipment? The more specifically one schedules an activity, the more likely it is to occur. Some couples guard against short memories by writing down their agreements.

Up to now, we've dealt with the problems that arise when she pushes and you pull; when he zigs and you zag. But there are those couples who reached the point of wanderlust together. And, once away from the pressures of juggling office, home, and who knows what else, they remembered what it was that brought them together in the first place. That's exactly what happened to Arnie and Fern Zipursky, the Toronto film producer and his social worker wife.

"Those four months were especially good for our marriage because we were completely on our own," said Arnie Zipursky. "We didn't even know the language, so we really had to lean on each other. I'll always remember it as a very intimate, very nurturing time."

CHILDREN

Is it fair to disrupt childrens' lives in order to indulge your own fantasies?

Without exception, this is the thorniest issue for parents when deciding whether to take a sabbatical away from home. No matter how committed they were to a trip, almost every parent confessed to some intense soul-searching when it came time to pull their kids out of school and away from their home.

"We thought about it long and hard," said Zeke Wigglesworth, whose children were 7 and 11 when the family spent six months sailing down the Mississippi River to the Bahamas in a boat they built themselves. "We couldn't afford to buy a boat, so we decided to build a thirty-eight-foot catamaran. We were very naive . . . neither of us had ever built anything larger than a bookcase."

The boat, which they thought could be completed in twelve months, ended up taking almost five years before it was seaworthy. To finance the trip, Wigglesworth sold his house, car, and every other worldly posession, except for his wife's piano.

"By that time, we had sunk so much time and money into the project that we just couldn't back out. Meanwhile, I was becoming more and more burned out at work, but I would come home and see the sailboat and it would just keep me going. Through it all, I was sure of the dream, but I was less sure about the kids.

"They worried that they would miss their friends and that they would fall behind in school, but when we returned they tested higher than ever. Five years later, they still talk about the experience. The trip was a very important piece of their education."

They also returned with the kind of knowledge you can't get in a classroom. "The kids learned how to navigate a boat and pulled kitchen duty once a week, just like the adults," he said, with more than a touch of paternal pride. "We went into the experience as seven individuals and came out a crew. We faced engine trouble, power failures, and ghastly weather and found out that we could meet the challenge. Most important, the kids came out of the experience with a better perception of what the real world is like—and that not everyone lives in a subdivision, wears designer clothes, and has a two-car attached garage."

In a sense, Wigglesworth's children had been living with the trip during the entire five years when the boat was being built in their own two-car, attached garage. When the time came to set sail, they knew they were ready.

Departures are not always that easy, particularly when they involve teen-agers and their friends.

"There were a lot of tears," said Charles Gusewell, describing the scene in June 1984, when he, his wife, and two daughters—then 14 and 15—left Kansas City for a year in Paris. "But at some point, you have to be the general. You must be the one to say, 'Trust me, this is going to be all right.' By October, they were crying at the prospect of having to return home. They went from stumbling, schoolgirl French to fluency; from a homogeneous midwestern high school to the American School in Paris, attended by students from fifty-two countries. They understand that they are citizens of the world."

So successful was the Gusewells' first experience that they repeated it in the summer of 1986; this time in Senegal and for four months instead of twelve. "I figured that this was our last summer to be together as a family, that I had one last shot with them before they're off on their own. I had to grab it."

Many psychologists advise that the time for a move is when the children are younger rather than older. Generally, parents don't have to be as concerned with the adjustment of children under five years old. Preschoolers are not tied in to settings as much as they're tied in to people. For them, home is where their parents are.

Adolescence, on the other hand, is a time when children pull away and become more independent of their family. In a foreign country, family members have to rely on each other more as a source of support. If a family is not functioning well, this can create conflicts.

For Jeremy and Rebecca Feinstein, ages 14 and 11, respectively, seven months in Israel posed no particular problems.

"At the time, they were not that involved with sports or after-school activities, so it was pretty easy," said Sue Feinstein, an audiologist. "They regarded it as an adventure. How your children react has a lot to do with their previous travel experience, their flexibility, and their attitude towards life in general. If it's open and expansive, they'll be eager. People forget how resilient children are. We recently discussed taking a couple months to go

England and Scotland and the kids piped in with 'Can we go? Can
we go?' That is not a typical response for teen-agers. But they have
been bitten by our love of travel. Usually, it is the children who
have traveled the least that are most resentful."

Since a miserable child can make for a miserable leave, what
steps can you take to make sure that your child belongs to the
former group rather than the latter?

"A lot has to do with the child and the type of sabbatical
you're taking," said Dr. Victoria Lavigne, a clinical child psychologist and assistant professor at Northwestern University. "If you
have the kind of kid who adapts easily and you're going to an
English-speaking country, it could be the experience of a lifetime.
But if you have an extremely withdrawn child and are going to
a place where people speak a different language, it could be a real
blow."

Dr. Lavigne offers these suggestions:

• How involved should children be in the decision-making
process? "Of course that depends on the age and the child himself.
If this is a child who is very tied to his peer group, it could be
difficult, but remember—a parent has a lot more knowledge and
experience than even an older adolescent."

An exception would be if a child got accepted into a special
program—for example, a music or sports camp. "Then you would
have to weigh the benefits of the leave versus the benefits of camp.
Parents shouldn't base their plans on a child's whims, but they
also should take their needs into account."

• In many overseas locations, you will find the same organizations that you find at home (such as Scouting and Little
League). If you are going to be in one place for an extended period,
these will give your child an instant peer group and help establish
a familiar routine. If you're in an area that is accustomed to
transient families (a university town or near a military base),
newcomers are old hat.

Regardless of the child's age, you need to present the temporary change as concretely as possible, said Dr. Lavigne. "That
means soliciting their ideas and involving them in the decision-

making process, getting out maps, looking at photographs, collecting guide books, making a game out of international road signs and talking to others who have been there."

• While a sabbatical is not a magic wand to be waved over relationships, several families reported strengthened bonds. Said one New York mother about her 15-year-old daughter: "For one year, she was away from the TV, the telephone, and the VCR. She *had* to talk to me."

GOING SOLO

Tom Doerk, 36, is the textbook case of the overachiever. He graduated with honors from Princeton University and Wake Forest College Law School. After weighing several job offers, he joined the Chemical Bank in New York. Seven years later, he was living in a teepee.

"All my life, I had been goal-oriented. In high school, the goal was to get into a good college, then a good graduate school, then a good job. Even though the pressure was intense, I could always count on summers off to relieve some of the stress."

But when Doerk said good-bye to his student status, he also said good-bye to three months of relaxation.

"I always took exotic vacations, backpacking through Europe or Australia. I moved around with the Chemical Bank—first getting transferred to San Francisco and then the Los Angeles office, before ending up at Northwest Bank in Minneapolis—but it wasn't the same. I needed more time for myself than work could give me. I yearned to be outdoors. Even with a four-week vacation, you're still looking at the calendar . . . the office is still blocking your view."

Doerk went looking for solitude—and he found his answer in a rather unlikely place: the *Wall Street Journal.*

"I knew I wanted to live with nature, but I didn't have the necessary skills to build a cabin. Then, right on the front page, I saw this article on teepees. I knew that was how I wanted to live for a significant amount of time. . . . The reactions from my co-workers ranged from horror to envy. The higher I went in the organization, the more encouragement I got. It was at my level that people were aghast."

After two years of preparation, Doerk pitched his tent in the desolate stretches of central Idaho, near White Bird (population: 50), and about as far from the pressures of banking as one can get.

Not everyone would embrace such solitary confinement. Whether you are traveling alone for just a few months or your single status is more permanent, many people have an overriding fear of loneliness.

If you're spending six months putting an addition on your house or a semester studying at a university, loneliness is not an issue. At home, your usual group of friends will continue to be a source of support; at school, your student status automatically makes you a part of something. But when you travel alone, you're not really a part of anything. Or are you?

Catherine Watson, travel editor at the *Minneapolis Star and Tribune,* while traveling alone across the Soviet Union met another single woman doing the same thing. "We traded experiences, particularly how people had said to us, 'You're so brave.' We had each told them, 'What could happen to me? It's just the world.' "

Such a plucky attitude is commendable, but not everyone—try as they may—is going to exhibit similar bravado. The rest of us worry about dining alone, of striking a confident pose while sitting at a French café *sans* companion, of trying not to look self-conscious when we approach the box office and say "one, please."

"You don't decide to go to the most remote corner of the world," said Watson, who took a year off in 1976 to live in South America. "You break it into little bits. You don't sit down on a Tuesday and decide to change your entire life by the weekend. You do it as you go along and as you feel comfortable."

Jeff Langer, a researcher at Bell Laboratories, wasn't comfortable at all when he planned his around-the-world sojourn in 1982. "So I built in a safety net. I arranged my itinerary so I would spend the first four months of my leave in Europe, where, if necessary, I could be home within twenty-four hours. Just that knowledge made me feel very secure."

Langer didn't cut his trip short. Instead, he went on to spend another seven months in India and the Far East. He met up with an acquaintance in Milan for a few days, but other than that, all his friendships were new ones. "I had always thought of myself as shy, but it was surprisingly easy to meet people. I found out that my shyness was a misconception. Learning that alone was worth the leave."

There are merits to both sides of the companion issue. Traveling with someone brings some security, economy (splitting expenses), and insurance against loneliness. On the down side, it can curtail spontaneity (you can't change the itinerary at a moment's notice) and a willingness to meet the locals. In addition, conflicts on trips—particularly long ones—can erupt over the most innocuous habits. Two colleagues almost parted company after a week of driving around the United Kingdom. Every time one man saw a cow, he could not resist the urge to break into a loud, bellowing "Moooo," much to the annoyance of the other.

Mark Ugowski, the Florida architect who traveled throughout the United States in 1984 remembers feeling alone, but not lonely. "My car broke down in Pittsburgh. I started talking with this bartender, which probably wouldn't have happened if I had been with someone else. The bartender took pity on me and kept filling up my glass. Eight beers later, I decided I could handle anything—including a busted transmission—but when I tried to pay, the bartender wouldn't take a cent. Traveling has a way of reaffirming your faith in the basic goodness of people." (The transmission, however, remained in need of repair.)

When you are staggering under a mountain of work and the office telephones are going berserk, the prospect of a deserted South Pacific island sounds very attractive. How do you know if you're really cut out for traveling alone?

Said Watson, "If you're a person who can be at home alone comfortably, go for it, because you will be rewarded. Even if you're going somewhere where you don't speak the language, you will make friends—and make them quicker—than you would at home. But if you have to break your arm—or heart—to do it, you're not ready. The price shouldn't be so high that you're homesick."

As for Tom Doerk, who is now back on banking's fast track, he found out that solitude is comforting—to a point. "I learned that I needed to be with people to be mentally stimulated. For the first time, I'm more comfortable in the corporate structure. Prior to the trip, my focus was diffused. I was spending half my time wondering what I was doing with my life and the other half doing my job. After Idaho, I knew I was in the right place."

Other tips:

• Take some small trips and see how you do on your own before you plan a seven-continent, fifty-two-week blitz.

• Traveling with a guitar, a harmonica, a backgammon, chess, or checkers board is an excellent way to break the ice. European train passengers are famous for sharing food, wine, and various contraband with total strangers.

• Don't feel that you must choose between traveling solo or with a companion. You can get the best of both worlds by alternating between the two—say, a few weeks with a tour or a cruise, followed by some time traveling alone.

• A job—whether it's paid or voluntary—is an excellent way to meet people. On the kibbutz, we lived, worked, ate, and socialized with the same people for virtually six months. The resulting friendships were far more intense than anything I had ever experienced in the "real" world. During our stay, many single volunteers arrived, finding the camaraderie a good antidote to their wanderings.

• Not everyone is going to have your luxury of time, but that doesn't mean that good friends can't rendezvous for a week or two. Your departure may be the impetus for someone else's vacation. (Could you resist an invitation by someone with a beach rental?)

• If you have a best friend you're leaving behind (or perhaps you're the one that's left on shore), the feelings can be unsettling. The person on leave is afraid of being forgotten: "What if we grow apart? What if our weekly lunches become a thing of the past—or I'm replaced by that n'er-do-well in accounting?" The person at home is worried about seeming dull after world travel or paling in comparison to the fellow Fellows.

With friends, as with family, the best bet is to meet the problem head on. Discussing your fears openly will go a long way and give each of you an opportunity to reassure the other. Also, being a faithful letter writer and making an occasional phone call helps keep close friends close.

• If the idea of traveling alone just doesn't sound appealing, there are some organizations to help singles find traveling companions. They include:

Travel Companion Exchange
Box 833
Amityville, N.Y. 11701

This organization helps people find compatible travel companions by matching up like applications, which covers everything from smoking to sightseeing. The membership fee is $4 per month (with a six-month minimum) plus a $5 initiation fee.

Travel Mates International, Inc.
49 West 44th St.
New York, N.Y. 10036

This agency plays matchmaker for singles with similar destinations rather than similar personalities and habits. Membership is $15 per year.

Companions in Travel
550 Jerusalem Ave.
North Bellmore, N.Y. 11710

This is another agency that depends on a personal profile to match companions. It also organizes group trips for single participants several times a year.

February 23, 1985

Dave and I stole a day for ourselves. We waited almost an hour in a driving rainstorm for a bus to Jerusalem. By this time, my clothes were soaking wet and my shoes were squishy. We took refuge in the Israel Museum, where we saw the Dead Sea Scrolls and a searing photography exhibit of Eastern European Jewry during the 1930s. A decade later, this entire world would be gone.

After a surprisingly good Chinese lunch, Dave returned to the kibbutz and I traveled on to Tel Aviv. I sat next to an interesting woman who works for the Jerusalem Post. Just when I thought I was sounding like a native, I took a taxi from the bus station and got ripped off on the fare.

The day ended on an up note, however, when everyone came back to our apartment for popcorn and a game of Scrabble. We all stayed up talking until 2 A.M. The last time I did this was in 1973. How fortunate we are to relive a part of our lives we thought was long over.

After everyone left, Dave asked what we will do if, by the end of our leave, one of us wants to stay here permanently. I honestly don't know, but I do know that the things we love best—family, friends, theater, movies, restaurants—are missing from kibbutz life. It is easier for us to take the good things about the kibbutz, such as the simplicity and the shared sense of purpose, and fold them into our old life than the other way around.

March 3, 1985

This weekend, we traveled three hours south to visit another kibbutz, located near Eilat.

We were staying at an apartment that was vacant because the tenants are on sabbatical—in Detroit, no less. Here, where "commuting" means walking to the dining hall.

If I left Israel today, I would return with the firm belief that anxiety is self-inflicted. Certainly, there are people at the office who are unaffected by the lurching from crisis to crisis, just as there are people on the kibbutz who carry Filofax appointment books and have a meeting every night of the week. It is up to each individual to monitor the stress and to turn it down like a thermostat.

March 20, 1985

Like stress, "office" politics are inescapable. Who gets what work assignments (women routinely end up with traditional jobs—kitchen, laundry, nursery, etc.), negotiating time off, and other special considerations almost always involve a confrontation with someone, which is disillusioning. In this community of 600, you think every one will be committed and sensitive, with moral compasses firmly in place. You quickly realize that a kibbutz is a community like any other community—no better, no worse.

April 2, 1985

I have been transferred to the orchards this week, which is harder than the laundry, but at least the time passes quicker. The oranges must be harvested by the end of the week and many of the kibbutzniks who usually work here are in the army. (Men must do two months of military service each year until the age of 55.)

I quickly found out that no one cares where you went to school, what newspaper you write for, or how many awards you've won. All they care about is if you can get to the crops before the rain does.

3

The Escape Hatch

Johnny Carson can take four months of vacation a year because he makes millions for NBC. John McEnroe's on-court antics are tolerated because the tournament sponsors need him. The rock group Van Halen has an M&M clause in their contract (ensuring a bowl of M&Ms in their dressing room, with the brown ones removed) because they're a box-office draw.

Clearly, you can get away with just about anything if you're good enough at what you do.

As much as we may want to believe otherwise, there is no democracy in the workplace. Who gets merit pay, vacations, corner offices, high-profile projects, parking places, and, indeed, personal leaves may have more to do with the studio star system than any tenets of the Constitution. Even unions cannot guarantee that perks are meted out equally.

So, if your company has no official leave policy and you think it would never grant one, think again: it may all depend on who is doing the asking. Of the seventy-five companies that I studied, a handful offer paid sabbaticals; at the other end of the spectrum, another handful reject the concept entirely. But the great majority responded with "Each case is evaluated on its own merits."

If an employee whose contributions to the firm range from marginal to invisible requests a leave, management will probably see this as an excellent opportunity to show him the door. But if an outstanding performer, who generates new clients, makes money for the owners, brings prestige to the company, and generally has a long list of successes to his credit makes the same request, do you really think management will risk losing him—especially to a competitor—by saying no?

Not a chance.

The annals of business are filled with stories of companies that went to great lengths to make sure that their stars would not be tempted by any rival offers.

When T. R. Reid, a highly-regarded *Washington Post* reporter, was being courted by the *Wall Street Journal* in 1984, *Post* editor Benjamin Bradlee offered to create a Denver bureau so that Reid and his family—avid hikers and skiiers—could spend more time on the slopes. Reid knew what he was worth—and so did Bradlee. Which brings us to the first rule of negotiations:

The only successful negotiations are the ones where everyone is a winner. "Don't get hung up on what the other side gets," said Gerard Nierenberg, founder and president of the Negotiation Institute, which organizes some 100 seminars a year on the subject. "What's really important is that you get what you want out of the deal. Try to find a solution that gives your opponent what he wants, while at the same time you get what you want."

Bradlee got exactly what he wanted—to keep Reid at the *Post*—and Reid got the Rockies in his backyard. Both sides were winners because they got something they valued. Outstanding employees are valued, respected, appreciated, and even cherished. All those nights that you worked until 10 P.M., all those weekends when you were knee-deep in paper while your colleagues were knee-deep in the surf, are now like money in the bank—and it's up to you to collect.

Many management experts believe that negotiating power has gradually tipped in favor of experienced employees. Employee turnover has become increasingly expensive to employers, and, as usual, nothing speaks as loudly as the bottom line.

"If a company can reduce its turnover rate, they can reduce their costs trememendously," said Robert Letering, coauthor of *The 100 Best Companies to Work for in America.*

"Every time a new employee comes in, the company has to make a sizable investment. Not only are there the obvious costs of recruitment and training, but there are intangible costs as well. When a valued employee leaves, a company has to reconsider how long it will take to get back up to speed. What does it cost if that employee takes some important customers with him? And, unless you're turning widgets on an assembly line, you're breaking up the team and that can effect morale. That, in turn, can affect productivity and how people feel about the company in general. When you take all that into consideration, it's just a lot easier to keep a valued employee happy."

Competition certainly explains why there are a large number of companies in the Silicon Valley offering paid sabbaticals, but few in Detroit. (As early as 1963, the United Steelworkers got extended vacations, when senior workers could take thirteen weeks paid leave every five years. Financially troubled steel companies scrapped the benefit in 1983.)

"It's a keep-up-with-the Joneses benefit," said one personnel manager for a high-tech firm. "It's a very expensive perk, which was fine when times were fat, but now it's a real drain on the company. I think, if given a choice, we would eliminate it, but we're all waiting to see who will blink first. We don't dare because that would give the others guys an edge and make us vulnerable to being raided. No one wants to lose their stars."

Which brings us to the second rule of negotiations:

Know thy worth. Negotiating is selling, but you can't sell unless you know what a commodity is worth. You probably know the value of your car or house, but have no idea of what your market value is to your employer. Time and again, company spokesmen say that they were willing to up the ante in compensation negotiation with employees, but most people underestimate their worth and are all too willing to settle for less.

Negotiating is no time for modesty. This is the time to emphasize how many new clients you've brought to the company, how many new products you've launched, or how many awards you've won. Unfortunately, in the business world, memories can be short. All too often, people forget how you closed up an expensive loophole or sweet-talked an irate customer out of bolting to the competition. It is difficult for most managers to remember yesterday's crisis because they're so absorbed with whatever crisis is currently unfolding. But if you've hit your share of home runs, now is the time to jar some memories. And if you can enlist someone else to toot your horn, even better.

Before you test the sabbatical waters with your boss (we'll discuss just how to do that later in this chapter), schedule a reality check. Make certain that you don't have some overinflated sense of your importance to the company. Don't wait for your annual performance review to solicit feedback. By identifying your deficiencies, you can tackle them immediately, so that you will be absolutely certain that the right people are pleased with your performance when D-Day arrives.

Said Richard Bolles: "Think of your employer's attitude as a curve that progresses from 'I like you' to 'I love you' to *'I've got to hold on to you.'* That's the only grounds on which to conduct negotiations."

And if you're not a star? Does that mean that the nose goes back to the grindstone? Not necessarily. As Woody Allen said, ninety percent of life is just showing up. Some steady performers have been able to parlay longevity and loyalty into a leave.

"How do you negotiate?" asked Charles Gusewell, a twenty-year-veteran of the *Kansas City Star.* "You stay long enough at one place, with one company and you make the kind of contribution so that your well-being is of some importance to them. If you've been at one job a year, no one is going to care whether you are refreshed and renewed, but if you've demonstrated a commitment, the power over your own life can increase tremendously."

Gusewell requested—and was granted—permission to write his column from Paris instead of Kansas City. To support his case, he could point to several factors. His popularity with readers, his

ability to relate to them whether he was sitting in the office or at
a café on the Champs Élysées, and his years of service. The editors
could not go out tomorrow and hire someone who had two
decades of experience in observing the local scene. But if a cub
reporter made the same request, they would probably show him
the door.

"To be in any kind of bargaining position, you have to pay
your dues. When you make this kind of investment, there are some
payoffs."

Given the number of mergers and acquisitions in today's marketplace, company loyalty as a career strategy has gone out of
vogue. Longevity alone should never warrant special favors, but
when teamed with talent, it can carry some weight at the bargaining table.

Do your homework. Some people just seem to have a knack for
knowing what's going to happen at work before anyone else. They
predict the hirings and firings, the buying and the selling, and
generally read the power signs like tea leaves.

This inside knowledge has nothing to do with clairvoyance and
has everything to do with enterprise. Taking advantage of information that most of us have access to—such as annual reports,
quarterly updates, stockholders' meetings, trade publications—
can be a gold mine. Knowing how corporate resources are al-
located can guide you in making your pitch, in knowing what
to stress and what to downplay, in what to ask for and what to
forgo.

Come armed with facts, particularly any bottom-line benefits
to the company. If you're proposing an unpaid leave, calculate
what saving your salary and benefits will return to the company
till. (According to the U.S. Chamber of Commerce, for every $1
American companies spend on salary, they kick in another 37
cents in benefits.) If last summer was a slow period and you want
this summer off—and you have the data to back it up—then be
sure to emphasize that in your proposal. If you know from the
grapevine that someone in another department took a leave—and
it was successful—then make sure your supervisor is aware that

a precedent has been set. (Some managers are reluctant to be trailblazers.)

If you are the first to propose a personal leave, then take your cue from those who may have gone on parenting or educational leave. The issue should not be whether or not you have a baby, but how the department can plan efficiently and function in a colleague's absence.

While data collecting usually means facts and figures, it's also important to look beyond the financial reports to grasp the more intangible information, such as corporate attitudes and priorities. What pushes your company's hot button? If it's voluntarism—which is held in high esteem at Control Data, Xerox, and Wells Fargo—perhaps you can work a volunteer stint into your leave. Other corporations have soft spots for education, the arts, or urban renewal.

When searching for solutions, don't forget to look outside your own backyard. Have other companies been able to use liberal benefits not only to retain good people, but to recruit them? This could be a particularly strong selling point if your organization is losing out to your competitor for top job applicants. "Good publicity attracts good people," said Nancy Thompson, vice president for Wells Fargo & Co., which offers a limited number of paid "personal growth" sabbaticals. "It creates good feelings within all our constituencies—not just customers and employees, but the community, as well. It's a win-win situation."

By starting a file with magazine and newspaper articles that report on companies with progressive human-resource practices, you'll be accomplishing two goals: accumulating data and establishing proof that the private concerns of employees can have very public results. Of course, all the documentation in the world doesn't mean top management will rush out and implement new policies, but, at the very least, they will be impressed with the scope of your research.

And if there isn't any data? Then create your own. Neil Glick, a lawyer in the Boston office of Sonnenschein, Carlin, Nath & Rosenthal, formed a sabbatical committee and sent out a survey to twenty-one law firms that already had leave policies in place.

He found out that one of the biggest fears—that an employee's absence will result in a drain on the firm's financial resources—was cited as a problem by only one respondent.

The worst time to learn new facts is when the negotiation is in progress—and returning to the bargaining table later with additional information severely weakens your case. You have to figure that you have one time—and one time only—to make your pitch; so make it count.

"Never let the other side be your only source of information," Neirenberg said. "Come as close as you can to reading their minds." (Always a useful skill for dealing with bosses.) "If you're operating from a position of knowledge rather than intuition, you will be operating from a position of strength."

THE PERSUASIVELY PENNED PROPOSAL

When most people think of negotiations, they think of verbal jousting. But your first round should be delivered in written form—namely, the memo. Not just any memo, but one that is just the right combination of eloquence, brevity, political astuteness, and timing.

Knowing when and where to direct your memo—essentially, your first official notice that you want time away from the office—is crucial.

First, the when: Before the ball can really get rolling, you have to know how amenable the boss is to your plans.

It is impossible to recommend an arbitrary schedule because so much depends on how you'll be spending your time off. If you are going to be returning to school, then you will need more lead time than someone who will be painting at home. Applying for a visa, finding a tenant, and storing your furniture are all steps that can add months to the getaway preparations. So, generally, the earlier you pitch, the better.

Plenty of advance notice not only gives you more time to get your personal affairs in order, but your professional ones as well.

Whether it's training a replacement or finding someone to service your clients in your absence, the more lead time, the easier the transition. (More discussion of this will follow in "Defusing Your Boss's Fears.")

Now, for the where: Even if your timing is impeccable, you can unnecessarily ruffle some feathers by sending your memo to the wrong person.

Do you risk sending it to your immediate supervisor out of respect for the hierarchy, even though that person may not be your staunchest ally and may even sabotage your request? Or do you go over his or her head in order to increase your chances for a favorable ruling?

In the great majority of cases, the second strategy makes more sense.

Enlisting the support of someone who may not support you—indeed, may even hinder you—is shooting yourself in the foot. Why play it so completely by the book when, if the proposal is rejected, there's a good chance that you may be leaving anyway? Do everything to stack the deck in your favor. If your immediate boss sees your move as a political taboo, you won't be around to deal with it anyway.

Should you make copies for other people affected by your decision? For the initial memo, I would advise against it. You don't want to trust this decision to a committee. But once the plans start to gel, you might send copies to all the appropriate people. A "cc" list (paying close attention to the chain of command) can be, depending on the politics of your particular workplace, good public relations.

Of course, while you may need to stick to the company's formal lines of power when you present your case, you certainly don't need to be so restrictive while you're building it. You should enlist the support of the informal power structure. If you have an ally a few notches up the organizational chart—perhaps a former boss who now heads up a completely different division—sound him or her out. Is there someone in your past who hired you? Who headed up a committee on which you served? Who got you a promotion? Ask their advice about the best approach. You never know who drives, lunches, or golfs with whom.

Now that you've identified who gets the memo when, what are you going to say in it? There's only one absolute rule: Do not approach this task with a chip on your shoulder. No matter how wrung out you are, don't let it seep into your memo. You want to convey an image of vitality and enthusiasm; someone who is out to embrace the world, not retreat from it. Wrack your brain to come up with some payoff for the company, but do stop short of total fiction. (Proposing that you will use your time off to conduct solar experiments when you'll really be perfecting your tan is ill-advised.)

Take pains to use words like trust, energy, and productivity (as in "I feel sure I will return with increased energy and productivity"). Anyone who has ever written a cover letter knows which words ring true and which ones hit the ear wrong. There is a difference between saying you want to shut out the world and read romance novels and saying you want time for contemplation and study.

Other tips:

- Keep it short, preferably to a single page. Hefty documents are the ones that always seem to get shuffled to the bottom of the pile. Write clearly and concisely and you will be twice as effective in half the space.
- Substantiate any claims with facts and figures. Experts cite unbacked statements as the most common mistake in business writing.
- Proofread for spelling and punctuation errors. If you present a proposal riddled with errors, what mistakes will you overlook when you leave?
- Establish a deadline. Some managers "manage" by moving everything to a back burner, so to expedite matters indicate that you would like some kind of response (such as scheduling a meeting for further discussion) by a specific date.
- In rare circumstances a memo may be inappropriate. If you work in a very small office or share a deep friendship with your boss, a memo—at least initially—could seem stiff and cold. A

"let's run it up the flagpole" discussion (to be followed by the requisite paperwork) would be more consistent with your relationship. Let past experiences be your guide.

Below is a sample memo:

> To: John Smith
> From: Bonnie Rubin
> I would like a year's leave of absence to study and live on a kibbutz in Israel, starting January 1, 1985.
> My family and I have been accepted to a program where my husband will be able to lend his architectural skills to a developing community on the West Bank.
> We see this as a rare opportunity to experience a foreign culture, learn a new language, and travel throughout Europe and the Middle East. I will gain a wealth of knowledge that will serve me well as a journalist. In short, we view this a chance to grow healthier—physically, mentally, and spiritually.
> During the last seven years I feel I have made many contributions to the paper including launching the new fashion section and winning several awards. I am quite confident that I have much more to offer this company in the future.
> Because I have many personal arrangements to make, I would like some indication of your feelings regarding this matter by October 1.

The ball is now in the boss's court.

DEFUSING YOUR BOSS'S FEARS

For negotiations to progress smoothly, your self-interests must mesh with the company's. "Search for common objectives," said Gerard Neirenberg. "Find all the ways in which you are alike, rather than ways in which you are different, and you'll have cracked the code."

Your boss wants to make sure the office will run smoothly while you're away, and you want the same thing. That already gives you a giant common objective.

Before you make your proposal, systematically list every potential problem that you can see arising from your absence. (A list of objections—and how they are defused—can be found on pages 94–95.) These rejoinders should not be included in the initial memo, but reserved for later in the negotiations, when you are dealing with more nitty-gritty issues. You always want to start with the general concept and then move on to specifics. Nothing will slow down the negotiation process faster than getting bogged down in too many details too early.

An employer's first and most general concern will undoubtedly be: "Who will fill the void caused by your absence?"

Finding a suitable replacement from the ranks, for example, may not be your responsibility, but you can bet that your suggestions will be welcome—and will show that you're thinking about the company's concerns as well as your own.

Is there a deserving underling who knows the operations of your department backwards and forwards? Would this be a good time to train someone else in office procedures? Several people mentioned that this was one of the most persuasive arguments they could make.

"People retire and go on disability," said Boston attorney Neil Glick. "The more we know about each other's cases, the better able we are to step in and take over the reins in an emergency. Sabbaticals would demand more communication. When clients learn that Joe down the hall is also a good attorney, we'll be a better integrated firm rather than just a bunch of isolated practitioners."

Continuity is crucial to a smooth-running operation, and the savvy leave-taker will do everything to make sure that every loose end is tied up before departure. In many offices, skills and information are so specialized that if one person is missing, the whole machinery grinds to a halt. Abandoning a project in mid-stream was a particular stigma at Bell Laboratories, a factor that Jeff Langer took into consideration when he made his pitch for a year abroad. He arranged to get himself on a project that would run until his departure. It was important to him that people would remember that he saw the project through to the end.

Having received assurances that the office will run like a well-made watch, the boss's next concern will undoubtedly be: "How much of my own time will I need to devote to this?"

Richard Bolles faced this problem when a researcher wanted a few months off after a long-term relationship she was involved in ended unhappily. Bolles was certain that the office could not function in her absence. She convinced him that, even if she left tomorrow, he would still have to make a time commitment whether she left permanently or took a leave. She told Bolles: "You'll still have to hire and train someone and when I return, she still won't be up to speed. Not only will I be able to run rings around my replacement, but I'll be recharged and raring to go."

He knew that she was absolutely right.

LEAVE YOURSELF AND YOUR BOSS PLENTY OF OPTIONS

Skilled negotiators know that you always want to leave yourself room for a little swapping. That way, each person feels as if he drove a hard bargain.

Sharon Murrel, who had worked at Bell Laboratories for seven years, went into negotiations wanting a year off from her job to spend with her boyfriend in Belgium. When she told her boss, the color drained from his face.

She ended up with an arrangement where she works three days with an affiliated company in Belgium in a joint research project and two days at the University of Antwerp. She wanted to spend twelve months overseas, her supervisor said he could only spare her for six; they settled on nine.

Not only did such an arrangement put her on the right continent, but it allowed her to keep key benefits. "I decided I needed my medical insurance, my pension plan, and the date I started with the company to stay intact. I flat out stated my goal to my boss and asked, 'How can we achieve this?' Together, we found a way. That is pretty typical of the way things work around here. In the research department, Bell is in competition not only with other companies, but with universities. They know that talented people always have options."

Like Murrel, if your original proposal meets with some resist-
ance, back up and try a different approach. One marketing manager was turned down for six months of sheer play in London, but
when he presented it as a chance to study new markets he got the
go-ahead. One 38-year-old researcher for a large electronics
manufacturer desperately wanted six months off to spend some
time with his new daughter. When his request for a paternity leave
was turned down, he proposed tinkering with a new product—
from his garage. The leave was approved.

Last-Minute Hand Holding

One of the most commonly expressed boss anxieties, one
that usually comes after the leave is approved, is: "How do you
keep employees down on the farm, once they've had all this
fun?"

Well, you can't. There are no guarantees that an employee will
return after a leave of absence anymore than there are guarantees
that an employee will return after the weekend. Someone who
wants to leave the corporate fold will do so, whether office policies
are liberal or not.

At my newspaper, there was a data processor who was a
graduate of MIT. Her experience and knowledge gave the department she worked in a much-needed shot in the arm. The only
problem was that she wanted to take four months off in the Virgin
Islands. "We couldn't get along without her," said Lee Petty,
personnel manager. "But what do you get if you say no? An
unhappy employee who will eventually leave anyway."

She got the leave.

The data processor never returned from the Virgin Islands, but
Petty said he still wouldn't have done things any differently.
"Someone who is taking a chunk of time off is almost always
grappling with some life decisions," he said. "I'd rather be the
kind of company who assists with that decision-making. There's
risk every time you move into uncharted waters, but there's more
risk when you don't."

Other tips for face-to-face negotiation:

• Create a good climate. Will you be interrupted by phone calls? Secretaries? When you're making your pitch, try to have as much mastery as possible over the situation. Some people prefer a more relaxed, social atmosphere and are totally at ease asking the boss out for lunch or drinks. Others feel that the office is the only appropriate place to address serious job issues. There is no right or wrong answer, only what makes you feel comfortable.

• When you discuss your proposal with your boss, know exactly what you're going to say. Rehearse, if you have to, until it sounds smooth but not robotic. Speak confidently and firmly. Take pains to purge the flab from your speech (the "ers," the "ums") and the qualifiers. "This department could operate more efficiently" is more authoritative than "I think the department could probably operate efficiently."

• According to Gerard Nierenberg, people confer an inordinate amount of legitimacy on the written word. If you ask for a raise and your boss pulls out an official looking card from personnel and says. "I'm sorry, but you're already at the top of the pay scale," many people meekly back off. But whether it's the checkout time at a hotel or the advertised price of a refrigerator, it's not above being challenged.

Said Nierenberg: "People got together and set the price of that refrigerator. The price itself was the product of negotiation, perhaps between the marketing arm and the financial arm of the manufacturer. Anything that is the product of negotiation is open to re-negotiation."

So when a manager reaches for his benefits handbook and says, "Gee, we have a policy on maternity leave, educational leave, and military leave, but we don't have any personal leave," that doesn't mean that those policies are etched in stone. They did not come down from the mountain top; they came off the desk of a mere mortal. Someone set them and someone can waive them.

• Finally, once the terms of your leave are hammered out, get it in writing. The supervisor who promised you that your desk will indeed be waiting for you may jump somewhere else or get hit by

a bus. (The Chinese proverb "the faintest ink is better than the best
memory" is applicable here.) Documentation is the best protec-
tion.

Now it's time for a dry run. By anticipating your boss's objections, you won't be caught fumbling for a response. Here's a
mythical exchange between boss and employee.

Objection: Why should I let one of my best producers go for
three months?
Response: Because I want to stay one of your best producers.
I know that this time away will give me an opportunity to recharge
my batteries, to return with renewed enthusiasm for the business,
with fresh ideas and some new approaches to old problems.
*(The emphasis is that you, the employee, will be moving towards
a goal, not fleeing an intolerable situation.)*

Objection: Who will assume your responsibilities while you're
away?
Response: Terry has superb organizational skills and played a
big part in our bringing our last three projects in on time and
under budget. I think it would be an excellent time to try her out
as project manager. And, since her seniority is much less than
mine, there'll be about a $6,000 savings in salary.
*(Smart negotiating on several counts: 1) By having an alternate
plan, you show the boss that his concerns are your concerns. 2) You
readily give credit to a colleague, always a class act. 3) You point
out any bottom-line benefits to the company.)*

Objection: What makes you think she can handle it?
Response: She did a great job pinch-hitting while I was on
vacation last year. Besides, it wouldn't hurt us to have another
person who knows the status of the project and who can deal with
clients.
*(Confidence is contagious. If you express faith in a colleague,
chances are the boss will, too. Another score: gently pointing out the
value of having more than one person plugged into the operation.)*

Objection: How do I know there won't be any gaps?

Response: Before I leave, I'll make sure everything is in order. Terry and I will go over the status of each account and I'll train her on the new computer. Also, a lot of the clients already know her, but I'll take her around the next time I make the rounds, just so they have a face to go with the name and they'll be aware of the change.

(Another opportunity to let the boss know that you have tended to every detail and will leave nothing to chance. The willingness to train your successor shows, once again, that you're a team player. The subtle reminder that clients are already familiar with Terry reassures him that clients aren't being dropped on some stranger.)

Objection: You and Terry are two of my top people in that department. Why should I disrupt a well-oiled machine?

Response: So we can keep it well-oiled. People need new challenges, and this opportunity to join an archaeological dig is mine. It's a lifelong dream—one that I've had on the back burner since I was in college—and I would hate to pass it up. Also, it will give my spouse and I some much-needed time together.

(There's nothing sinister here. No threats that if my request isn't approved I may be tempted to look elsewhere. The reference to a lifelong dream has the sound of solid vision, rather than an impulsive act. From past conversations, you know the boss is a firm believer in marriage.)

Objection: If you take a leave, everyone will want to take a leave.

Response: A lot of people aren't financially able to take six months off and, even if they could, not everyone will have the desire. If it's successful with me, we can evaluate it when I return. Who knows? Maybe it will become a terrific recruiting tool and will be viewed as one of the benefits of being associated with our company. Why not try it out on me as a no-cost trial balloon?

(Pointing out that some employees won't be able to afford a leave hammers home the point that this arrangement doesn't cost; in fact, it may pay.)

If you were a fly on the wall, you would get the impression that both sides have come to the bargaining table to find a solution. The tone is measured, the logic is sound. Neither participant sounds accusatory or defensive. The leave is presented as a business proposal rather than a personal problem, meaning that the boss can view it as a manager, not as a social worker.

Other possible selling points that could have been used:

• Terry's increased responsibilities could free you up when you return, possibly for that pet project you know the boss has wanted to tackle, but just hasn't had the manpower.
• It will coincide with the office's slow season.
• You are willing to investigate some new markets while traveling.

As for agreeing to be available by phone, most people advise against it. "It's just too easy for someone from the office to call at the first sign of a problem rather than solving it themselves," said one buyer for an east coast department store. "If I had to do it all over again, I'd at least be in a different area code."

Jeff Greenfield, ABC's media and political analyst, was on leave when the Gary Hart–Donna Rice story broke and couldn't resist an invitation to appear on "Nightline." Said Greenfield: "I worked for 45 minutes. It was just too good to pass up."

AREN'T I INDISPENSABLE?

There is an underside to having a leave approved and that is the irrefutable evidence that the office can survive without you.

No one is indispensable. No matter how many victories you've chalked up, if you didn't show up tomorrow, life would go on.

Some people find this out the hard way—when a new boss brings in his own management team, when a company eliminates an entire department or just closes its doors for good. Everyone knows a sad story about some guy who dropped everything for the company, only to have the company drop him.

"People tell themselves that they're indispensable because

that's what they really want to believe," said Sue Mengas, who runs the Anxiety Clinic at the Hartford Medical Center. "What is expressed as a fear—that they'll never be able to get away and that the office will fall apart without them—is really a wish. A lot of people also have a competency problem—myself included—and should know better. That's when you put a tremendous amount of pressure on yourself to be perfect. We really see a lot of this around Christmas—patients saying 'I've got to bake, I've got to make the ultimate dinner, I've got to buy everyone perfect gifts, which have to be perfectly wrapped.' When you ask them why, the answer is invariably 'that's what my friends and family expect of me.' Well, that's what you put on yourself because that's what you think will get you love and approval. It's a very secure individual who does not try to be all things to all people."

Arnold Kanter, a Chicago lawyer, fits that description. After a leave in 1982, he found a more relaxed routine suited him just fine. He started with a leave and when he returned, he switched to "of counsel" status, meaning he decreased the number of hours he spent practicing law and increased the number of hours he spent reading, lecturing, and being with his family. Said Kanter: "I pride myself on my dispensability. I always thought it would be great to work for a firm that not only makes sabbaticals available but actually requires that they be taken. It says a lot about the level of trust within a firm."

So think of all the lunches you spent grabbing a sandwich at your desk, the theater tickets that went unused, and the vacations that were canceled. Then put any ambivalent feelings to rest.

WHAT ABOUT MY CO-WORKERS?

Depending on how aggressively office politics are played in your company, co-workers may have the power to make your last days uncomfortable.

First, acknowledge that offices live, breathe, and exist on predictability. Any time you upset the status quo, it can send shock waves through the organization—be it a small business or a megacorporation. Change—no matter how trivial, no matter how little impact it will have on an employee's life, no matter how many assurances of "you're going to love it"—never goes down easily and is always viewed as a potential threat.

The question that will loom in everyone's mind is "How is this going to affect me?" You're standing on the brink of an adventure; all they have to look forward to is more of the same—or worse. It's difficult for co-workers to share your enthusiasm when all they can see is that, for the next six months, there's a good chance they'll be coming in on Saturdays while you're on the Orient Express.

It is your job to allay those fears. To the best of your ability, share any information you have regarding how your leave will—or will not—affect their workloads. If the boss plans to hire a temporary or someone is going to step in from a different department, let them know. Just reassuring the troops that someone recognizes their concerns—and is already working on a solution—will go a long way in reducing hostility.

Once the word of your leave is out, expect some people to treat you as nonexistent.

The simple fact that you won't be around makes you a lame duck. The period between the time your leave becomes public and the time you actually depart is not unlike someone who has already given their two-week notice and will be taking another job. Any office recognizes that the important players are the ones who can make or break careers—and, at least for the time being, you do not figure in that equation.

But being *persona non grata* also comes from swimming against the tide. Psychiatrists who have studied organizational behavior say that there isn't much difference in the way a family responds to someone who deviates from the norm and how the office responds. Both are a matter of the individual versus the group, and both take a strong ego to stand up to. There's a continual conflict of wanting to belong to the group but also wanting independence.

In either families or offices you can count on a few naysayers who will tell you that you are committing professional suicide. It's usually under the guise of concern, something like "Aren't you afraid your department will learn to do without you?" or "Why would you want to do something like that?" Smile sweetly and think "So I don't have to deal with clods like you."

Far more hazardous is the office vulture, already circling overhead, eyeing your office and parking space. Is there anything you can do to protect your turf while you're gone?

Remind yourself that the vultures are always there, whether you are on the job or not. While it's true that you may not be able to watch your backside while you're out of the office, consider the pluses: While you won't be around to take the credit, neither will you be around to take the blame. It is almost a cliché in the business world that when a project goes haywire, there is always praise for the nonparticipant.

It is easy to feel powerless in office warfare, particularly if you're thousands of miles from the battleground, but sometimes the distance can turn out to be a well-timed buffer zone. One Chicago accountant, who was sailing during a corporate takeover, felt that his leave kept him safely out of the line of fire during a particularly stormy period. "I returned unscathed and unaligned with any of the warring factions. Because I was gone for so much of the bloodletting, I was perceived as totally neutral. I was welcomed back with open arms because I didn't see people at their worst."

Other leave-takers reported that their respective stocks went up just by being away from the day-to-day annoyances and petty disagreements that are part of any workplace.

One copywriter for a Los Angeles advertising agency who felt overworked and underappreciated thought his leave made it easier for management to see his contributions. "My immediate supervisor made a practice of taking credit for my ideas. She told me that when she was promoted she would take me along with her. Meanwhile, I felt as if I was getting the short end of the stick because I simply was not getting the credit I deserved. I took a semester off to return to school and when I returned I think the bosses had a much more accurate picture of what was going on."

Sometimes the changes are less concrete, more a matter of style over substance. A Los Angeles accountant, who took a leave to sail to South America, said his solo journey changed the way he was perceived by his employer.

"All of a sudden, I was seen as this courageous, unflappable guy rather than the wimp in accounting. It wasn't only because I was out there battling the elements for six months, but because I could walk away from the fast track. I detected a respect that wasn't there before."

Other tips:

• If you overhear someone complaining about your leave, remember that it isn't necessarily directed at you; it's a predictable nervousness that organizations go through every time there's a reshuffling.

• Don't respond to every criticism, but if you feel that patently untrue information may jeopardize your leave or your employer, squelch it immediately. One member of a United Way staff, who got a leave during a period of particular belt-tightening, was distressed to hear that the grapevine had her receiving half-salary. "Actually, I was given an unpaid leave—I didn't even get benefits. My absence wasn't costing a cent, but the rumor took on a life of its own. I put out a memo, detailing the conditions of my leave. Someone else might say that such action was overreacting, but I felt a need to set the record straight. If that erroneous information had leaked out, it would have been very damaging to the credibility of the organization."

• If you're a manager, be visible and accessible. One Los Angeles hospital administrator, who negotiated a year off as an extended maternity leave, found out that certain employees were circulating erroneous information—that in her absence, the department would be restructured and jobs would be phased out. Six months earlier, the hospital had started sharing some services with another neighboring health-care facility, and some people saw the administrator's temporary departure as a sign that she was bailing out. In an atmosphere already rife with apprehension, the rumors poured more oil on the fire. Instead of calling the rumor mongers on the carpet privately, she acknowledged the scuttlebutt at a staff meeting and reassured employees that the information was simply untrue.

• If you're troubled at the thought of being the subject of a co-worker's lunch conversation, tell yourself: 1) that you would be doing exactly the same thing if they were leaving, that 2) people gossip whether you leave or not, and that 3) nobody is liked by everyone. Very few people beyond high school devote their time and energy to winning popularity contests. If you think that the political ramifications of your sabbatical are going to give you that much angst, perhaps you should reexamine your motives. To use your time off to worry about the office is to totally defeat the reasons for going.

• Keep a sense of humor. Some people are always looking for a fight. If you're the object of some good-natured razzing, laugh it off. It's difficult for co-workers to feel resentful when something good happens to someone they admire.

• Finally, acknowledge that any transition creates feelings of ambivalence. It isn't just the "good-bye party" for a peer that can be unsettling, but the wedding, the awards dinner, and the baby shower as well. Such events force us to scrutinize our own timetables. Are we progressing at the rate that we should?

"Be aware that others are bound to be experiencing these twinges of wistfulness and tread softly," said Dr. Gale Levin. "Don't gloat or make your co-workers feel as if they're suckers for sticking around. Stress how this time off gives you more time with family, not how you can't wait to get away from this place—even if that's the way you really feel."

WHAT IF THE BOSS SAYS NO?

If your proposal is rejected, it really comes down to two choices: stay or quit.

Quit. The word comes out in a staccato burst. It sounds so harsh, so final. Depending on your point of view, it is either the ultimate irrational act or the ultimate act of heroism, done for all kinds of reasons and in all kinds of ways.

I have seen a fifteen-year veteran go on vacation one day and never come back. He didn't clean out his desk or attend the obligatory good-bye party. Instead, he just faded into the sunset. The payroll office sent him checks for three weeks before anyone noticed.

Some years later, I saw a distinguished editor, with thirty-years' seniority, resign rather than to obey a directive from the publisher to lay off employees. It was the first time I saw 150 jaded, hard-bitten journalists give a standing ovation. Both stories went on to become newsroom legends.

Stories of employees quitting—with nothing but uncertainty waiting in the wings—are retold with a mixture of envy, awe, and disbelief. Given the competitive nature of the job market and the vagaries of the economy, can anyone be so foolish—or so confident?

Many people choose to leave good jobs that give them salary, prestige, and power—everything but fulfillment—rather than stay and feel like a powerless pawn. The emotional roller coaster—of deciding to ask for a leave, of sweating out a response and finally being rejected—eventually screeches to a halt. When it does, most people do not experience remorse, but an odd sense of calm.

"The anguish was the time I spent vacillating back and forth," said a project manager for a Philadelphia construction company. "Once I made my decision, I really felt as if I was in control. That's something people tend to forget. That no matter what, you are ultimately the master of your fate."

One point is certain: To wrestle back that control, to show that you indeed have the ability to direct your own fortune, is a sign of health, security, and self-esteem.

If your leave request is turned down, career consultants overwhelmingly favor severing relationships rather than carrying on valiantly, like some spurned lover.

"If the answer is no, you'd better be prepared to submit your resignation, because it will be awkward for you and awkward for your company," said Richard Bolles.

"Everyone will know that you wanted to leave and you

couldn't; that your heart lies elsewhere. You will be operating in a goldfish bowl, with colleagues and managers watching and waiting to see what your next move will be, and that is a very uncomfortable situation."

Of course, this is simply not practical advice for everyone. First, not everyone has the option of quitting. Second, not everyone wants to.

You may be genuinely happy with your job, but just want to take a break from your daily routine. Now, all of a sudden, the boss says no and the stakes have escalated. Is this something really worth quitting over?

That depends. First, let's view the rejection in the proper context.

- Is this one more slight in a long line of slights?

Have you been passed over for several promotions? Have you repeatedly asked for a raise and been told "wait until next year"? When an important project comes along are you left off the team? Management may be sending you a message. The rejection of your request may be just what you need to see things as they really are, not as you wish them to be.

If, on the other hand, management has shown you on numerous occasions that you have a bright future with the organization, then parting company could be a foolish move. If you fall into this group, ask yourself:

- Is there another way to get the leave?

Before you throw away that memo, ask your boss what it will take to reach some middle ground. Perhaps all you need is a couple modifications (for example, shaving a month off your leave or being available by phone) to make it work. As long as the lines of communication are kept open, a ruling can still be made in your favor.

If the answer is still no, explore every conceivable option within the company. Will a transfer to a different office satisfy your urge for a change of scenery? If it's travel you crave, can you apply for another position, perhaps one that allows you to spend more hours out of the office? Try to tailor your job to fit your needs.

- Are you willing to live with the consequences?

If you miss the opportunity, will you regret it? Will it come around again or be gone forever? What are you risking by staying? What are you risking by leaving?

QUITTING

This is usually a last resort. Even though the handwriting may be clearly on the wall, many people choose to stay in near-debilitating situations, figuring that the known—be it an abusive boss or an unrealistic work load—is infinitely better than the unknown. Perhaps that is why, according to the latest Gallup poll, we have a work force where a mere 30 percent describe themselves as "satisfied" with their jobs.

Said Srully Blotnik: "You have to be sufficiently uncomfortable to take the plunge. However, the people who do leave their present jobs are, by and large, overwhelmingly glad they did, even if they get knocked around. At least they feel as if they are being propelled forward. It is the standing still that can be excruciating."

Voluntarily leaving your job can be viewed as insanity by colleagues—but it is no more insane than staying in a situation where you are miserable. Colleagues thought Lowell Cohn, a vice president for a New York advertising agency, was crazy for walking away from a $100,000 salary in the early 1970s. "I was vacationing in Europe and I got a call to return to New York for a meeting. I said, 'What do you need me for? To fill up a chair?' That's when I knew I would be leaving. I was able to remedy the problem by leaving the business. Very few people are willing to do that."

Like divorce and plastic surgery, unemployment—voluntary or otherwise—is not the taboo it once was. The average worker will change careers three or four times during the course of a lifetime. Gaps in employment histories or résumés are simply not that unusual anymore.

If you take a leave when you are in your 30s or 40s—the period that Blotnik considers the optimum time—you do not automatically revert to rookie status when you return. In fact, in a curious catch-22, it is experience that has caused you to seek challenges elsewhere. No one just starting out ever feels stale. It's only after you've been at it for a while that life seems all routine and no rewards.

It is a far more assertive strategy to leave your job gracefully, take the summer or year or however much time you want off, and then tackle job-hunting with renewed ambition. You're not throwing your career away, just putting it up on the shelf for a while.

Zeke Wigglesworth, now travel editor for the *San Jose Mercury News,* left his job rather than stay and be the good soldier. "I'll be the first to admit that I was looking for pure escapism," he said of his six-month cruise down the Mississippi River. "I was unhappy, so I built a boat and sailed away. When I left, I couldn't cope with anything. When I returned, it was with a sense of accomplishment and self-respect [and his old job]. Even if you have to quit your job, you still have your skills and knowledge, which no one can take away from you. If you were any good when you left, you'll be able to find a job when you return, but you may never have another opportunity for such a fulfilling experience. To me, that was certainly worth the professional sacrifice."

Sue Wolkerstorfer, who works in public relations for Control Data, was a member of the Wigglesworth crew and found that it never turned out to be the professional liability she had feared. "I probably got far more job interviews because people were intrigued by the trip on my résumé."

As long as they were careful not to bang the door too loudly on the way out, numerous leave-takers found that when they were ready to return to the work force, their old positions were still available. Tom Doerk, a loans officer, quit when his bank denied his leave request for six months off. "Actually, it turned out to be a blessing in disguise because a leave would have represented just one more deadline, which was precisely what I was trying to get away from."

Doerk took his time off and didn't miss a beat. He accepted his bank's decision and headed for central Idaho anyway. When he returned to Minneapolis, he was welcomed back with open arms—which says a lot, not only about the way Doerk worked but about the way he left. "I ended up with the same bank, the same desk, even the same business cards. Almost everything was identical—except that I got a raise when I was rehired."

No one can say that if you quit, your situation will end as happily as Doerk's. No one can unequivocally say that you should do this or that in a situation, because every situation is different. Even career counselors don't have all the answers.

Richard Bolles, then an Episcopal minister, was awarded a prestigious fellowship in Washington, D.C., but the governing body of the parish voted down his leave request. Immediately afterwards, he needed to channel his energy into the church's annual fundraising campaign. "I gave 150 percent," Bolles said. "One of the board members came up to me after my presentation and expressed unqualified admiration. After rejecting my request, he had just expected me to put forth a half-hearted effort. No matter how unfairly you think you've been treated, you will never regret taking the high road." (Bolles did quit, but not until after the campaign was completed.)

It may be an acting performance worthy of an Academy Award, but exhibiting a rekindled passion for work will never hurt, and will often help. Accept criticism willingly, volunteer for new projects, rise to the challenge of blooming where you are planted. When everyone expects you to respond one way and you respond another, you can still hang on to that all-important feeling of control. It lets you hold your cards close to your vest and puts the element of surprise on your side. Most important, if you refuse to wear a badge of self-pity, no one can cast you in the role of the hapless victim. Incessant whining, bad-mouthing the company, or adapting a "nobody appreciates me" attitude will not convince anyone that a terrible unjustice has been committed. Indeed, it will only reinforce management's decision that you are an albatross around the corporation's neck rather than a valued employee who deserves to be accommodated.

Other tips:

•   Do not issue ultimatums. No manager likes to have an employee force his hand. If you threaten to quit if your company rejects your leave, you may be forced to leap sooner rather than later.

•   Examine your reasons for staying. Frequently, people say they can't leave when what they really mean is that they won't leave. It's one thing to stay in an intolerable situation to put food on the table and another because you have seniority, generous vacation benefits, or a short commute. "Staying at one job too long is a commonly made mistake, particularly by women," said George Martelon, a Denver career counselor. "They often stay on, trying to change the attitudes that frustrate them and hoping things will get better. They rarely do."

•   Even though you may want to purge your memory of everything that has to do with your job, don't let your membership in professional groups and trade associations lapse. It's one of the best ways to keep up your contacts and stay plugged into the industry grapevine. When you're ready, these contacts may well be your bridge back to the working world.

•   Take solace in the stories of those who faced adversity and licked it. Inspirational tales of people who were fired and started their own companies are to business what the story of Lana Turner being discovered at Schwab's Drugstore is to starlets. While feeling stuck in a job is not the same as a having a terminal illness, thinking about it certainly can occupy most of one's waking hours. Had I not been cut from the Michigan program, I would have had no reason to seek my own leave and see the world. The symbol in Chinese for "crisis" is the same as "opportunity." They're on to something.

April 19, 1985

Probably the most significant event of the last week has been Holocaust Memorial Day. Our visit to Yad Vashem (the Holocaust Memorial in Jerusalem) burned an indelible image into my mind, especially the terse reminiscences of an SS soldier, describing his execution of a family: "There was never a cry for mercy. . . . A grandma tickled the foot of a baby, a father pointed upward to his young son. They were holding hands and smiling."

The next day, at 8 A.M., two minutes of silence were observed in memory of the martyrs. Everywhere, machinery abruptly shut down. The squabbling of the marketplace stopped. Cars and buses pulled over to the side of the road. For two minutes, the movement of an entire nation came grinding to a halt. I felt a special bond with the other women in the laundry as we shared this solemn moment. I looked over at Flori, but her face revealed no anguish over her own Bergen-Belsen experiences, only faith.

April 22, 1985

We're in a real honeymoon period right now. I don't know when I've felt so relaxed and healthy. I've forgotten about the problems that were plaguing me like migraines before we left.

Yesterday, Michael visited me at the laundry during his morning break. He sat on the end of the ironing board and talked while I finished some shirts. I sent him on his way and about two minutes later, he returned, clutching a small bouquet of flowers. It was straight out of a Hallmark commercial. Despite the picture of parenthood painted on TV, such warm moments are rare at home, perhaps because they don't have a chance to take root. It's either 7 A.M. and I'm hustling a half-asleep child out the door with a Styrofoam cup of Cheerios or it's 9 P.M. and I'm hustling a wide-awake child into bed with an abridged version of *Cinderella* and a peck on the cheek.

Can we hang on to some of the benefits once we return home, like more time and fewer toys—for all of us? During the last five months, we've been able to close a gap that was widening all the time. Despite what Helen Gurley Brown says, I doubt whether you can have it all—at least not at the same time.

It's ironic that I had to come halfway around the world to realize just how much satisfaction I get from my work. Most of the world's jobs are not only achingly tedious, but anonymous. Even if I did an outstanding job pressing a shirt, no one would know it—not even the owner. It took standing over an ironing board to realize just how much I need feedback.

April 24, 1985

Last night, there was a memorial service for sons of the kibbutz who had fallen in battle since 1948. It was brief, solemn, and, above all, poignant. In the dining room, photographs of the soldiers and meticulously maintained scrapbooks of their lives kept them perpetually young. All 300 members of the kibbutz snapped to attention as a siren sounded and the flag was lowered to half-mast. Then we all sang "Hatikvah" (the Israeli national anthem, which means "hope"). In the distance you could hear the wail of one siren after another, as each kibbutz remembered its own. Scarcely a person exists who has not lost a father, a son, or a brother to war. In contrast, we do not know a single person who even served in Vietnam, much less became a casualty. Until today, Veteran's Day and Memorial Day meant little more than a day off work and appliance sales. Here, people remember passionately.

April 25, 1985

Today we visited Ammunition Hill in Jerusalem, site of one of the bloodiest battles of the 1967 war. The soldiers who died there came alive to us through their carefully mounted biographies and letters. Amir's first-hand experiences enriched our visit. "After a *lifetime of living in a divided Jerusalem, we woke up one morning and saw the Israeli flag flying over the Old City and we cried."*

It was Ammunition Hill that ultimately won the reunification of Jerusalem. Today, old soldiers guide visitors through the small museum, where the names of the deceased are etched in granite. Outside, children play ball and families hold picnics on this same hill—which is perhaps the most eloquent memorial of all.

4

Money, Money, Money

When co-workers heard of my plans to swap my desk in Minneapolis for a tractor in Israel, their first questions were about money. They were certain we had just come into an inheritance or won the lottery. Unfortunately, neither was true.

There are almost as many ways to finance a leave as there are reasons for taking one. None are easy. It takes a lot of money to stage a getaway and it takes a lot more to get back on your feet when you return. But more valuable than a fat bank account is time, energy, and an unshakable view of yourself. You must be able to actually see the sun reflecting off the stucco and tile-roof houses of St. Thomas, you have to be able to hear the sound of water splashing against your boat and the feel of the soft breeze against your cheek. You have to be able to smell the soufflé as you whisk it out of the oven at Cordon Bleu Cooking School in London. You'll need all that mental ammunition to carry you over the inevitable setbacks you will encounter along the way.

"One of the saddest lines in the world is, 'Oh come now, be realistic,' " said Richard Bolles. "The best parts of this world were not fashioned by those who were realistic. They were fashioned by those who dared to look hard at their wishes and gave them horses to ride."

There are a variety of "horses" to carry your wish to the finish line, ranging from prestigious grants to old-fashioned frugality. You don't need to be well-heeled to finance a leave, but you do need to be well-planned. Having a comfortable budget buys you peace of mind, which, after all, is the reason you're going on sabbatical in the first place.

The next question is how do you define "comfortable"? For a privileged few, it will mean plush hotels and four-star restaurants. Other folks will be perfectly content to be living out of a knapsack and cooking beans over the campfire. It is impossible to determine your budget until you determine the nature of your leave and vice versa.

KNOW THYSELF

The two factors that will shape your budget are the length of getaway and the style in which you wish to travel—if you are traveling. Turn up the luxury and you may have to return to work sooner than you would like; on the other hand, don't create a budget so devoid of amenities that the chances of you adhering to it are about as good as Sylvester Stallone's playing Hamlet. If restaurants are important to you, don't plan a budget with the idea of eating freeze-dried food out of a pouch. It would be unrealistic to recommend a budget without knowing where you're going, how you're traveling, and if there is some housing (your biggest expense) available—as it was for us on the kibbutz. In the Middle East, $10 a day buys you some amenities; in New York, it barely buys lunch. Whatever your budget, know that it is only human nature to live precariously perched on the edge—not a good place to be, especially if you're half a world away from your friendly neighborhood bank.

SOURCES OF FUNDS (OR FUN)

According to Louis Lichtenfeld, vice president in the corporate finance division of Dean Witter Reynolds, Inc., financing a leave is not unlike starting a business. "There are ongoing expenses such as continuing housing payments, insurance, and taxes; there are also intangible expenses, such as building up good will with your employer through hard work and company loyalty. Either way, you have to pay a price for your freedom."

Before you clear out your desk, Lichtenfeld suggests asking yourself some key questions:

How long do you wish to be away? How much ready cash do you have? What will you need? How much money can be raised by the sale of noncash assets? What is the purchasing power (what will your dollar buy) at your destination? How many amenities are you willing to forgo? If you're going abroad, what is the inflation and exchange rate to the dollar? How much lead time do you need to accumulate the funds necessary for your sabbatical? What are your prospects for earning passive (nonsalary) income while you are gone? Most of these questions, of course, are answerable only by you. No one knows your spending habits better.

The next step is to practice some budget and cash-flow planning. It is imperative to consult an accountant or tax manual for more details on some of the following suggestions that involve tax strategies. Everyone's situation is different and there are often exceptions to the rule.

Each year between 1987 and 1990 will involve a sliding scale of rate changes and new limitations. Tax-planning assistance of some kind is likely. You can obtain Publication 553, highlighting these changes, free from the Internal Revenue Service.

Speeding up your cash flow by lowering your withheld taxes. You can bolster your take-home pay by reducing your withheld taxes while you're still on the job. Fill out a new W-4 Federal Tax Withholding Form for your employer increasing your withholding allowances and thus your take-home pay. Since you will be gone a portion of the year, your annualized earnings will be less (you are, in a sense, borrowing from Uncle Sam). Be very careful when doing this. Beginning in 1987, if you have not paid in 90 percent of your tax liability for the year, you may face interest and penalties. The longer you're gone and the higher your income, the more significant the strategy becomes.

Speeding up your cash flow by shifting your income. A desirable plan is to shift income to your sabbatical year from the years before or after your leave. This will lessen your salary fluctuation and reduce your overall tax bite. (Make sure that you make tax allowances for changes in your salary.)

Let's assume that you are single, with a taxable income of $30,000 a year, and wish to take the last eight months of 1988 to bicycle through Europe. You will work all of 1989 after returning from your leave. If your employer is agreeable, take a $10,000 "raise" from January through April of 1988—in other words, the four months that you are on the job prior to your departure. Upon returning in January 1989, you take a $10,000 pay "cut."

(Your employer will want some assurance that you will come back to work after giving you that $10,000 "raise." This can be accomplished by "loaning" your company $10,000 through payroll deductions during the period that you're working. Your company will repay your loan the year you return.)

In the example below let's assume that your salary is your taxable income.

CASE 1: Without income shifting plan:
1988— $10,000 (four months' work during sabbatical year)
1989— $30,000 (full-year earnings after sabbatical year)
Total: $40,000
Two-year tax liability: $7,507

CASE 2: With income shifting plan:
1988— $20,000 (four months' work during sabbatical year plus $10,000 "raise" by your employer)

1989— $20,000 (full year earnings after sabbatical year minus $10,000 "pay cut" from your employer)

Total: $40,000

Two-year tax liability: $6,623

Tax savings by using the income-shifting plan is $884 although this does not take into account any interest your employer may charge for the loan.

One more disclaimer: This strategy requires special attention. Advantages vary depending upon your salary, your filing status, and the tax years involved. Generally, the greater your salary, the less the benefits. Again, consult one of the aforementioned sources for help.

Tapping your retirement funds. If you're gone for a large portion of the year, consider borrowing from your IRA, profit sharing, or pension plan. You will be subject to an early withdrawal penalty and will probably be taxed at ordinary income rates on your IRA. However, your income relative to your normal annual salary will be significantly less, making the penalty not such a bitter pill to swallow. Again, the benefits are directly linked to the length of your stay and income level. For two months, it may not be worth jumping through so many financial hoops; for ten months, it could well be worth the trouble.

Better still is if your company has an employee stock bonus plan or company profit-sharing plan. There are even more options than are available through IRAs while avoiding the 10 percent penalty. They are:

1) Withdrawals may be made at any age because of retirement, termination, or hardship.

2) Borrowing is permitted if the loan is repaid within five years.

3) Lump-sum distributions may qualify to be averaged over five years for income-tax purposes. There are various qualifications of this rule that require more in-depth inquiry.

Many companies have profit-sharing plans in which they match all or a portion of your personal contribution. Every plan is different, but in almost all cases there is a maximum that you are eligible to contribute. In other words, don't expect to put your entire check into a profit-sharing plan with the idea that your employer is going to match it dollar for dollar.

The most important rule about profit-sharing and pension plans: The higher the income and the younger you are, the stronger the case for using your funds. However, said Lichtenfeld, "here the down side is that there are limitations on what you can actually get your hands on prior to retirement." The closer you are to retirement, the stronger the case for leaving funds untouched.

Here are two examples. In both cases, the leave-taker is 40 years old, earns $60,000 a year, and wants to spend six months at Martha's Vineyard during 1988 but still have the $30,000 that he would earn had he stayed on the job. Each has already accumulated $50,000 in a pension plan.

Case 1: Withdrawing $30,000 in one lump sum
Tax liability: $6,354
Case 2: Taking the full $30,000, but averaged over the next five years (in other words, $6,000 per year). The primary benefit: You are taxed on this $6,000 at the lowest rates.
Tax liability: $828 the first year

There are so many different variables (age, income, how much you're going to take out of your pension plan, what's left, how long the actuarial tables say you're going to live after retirement—and that's just for starters) that it is best to consult a tax lawyer.

Indeed, about the only points that can be stated without qualification are that under the new tax laws, the interest expense on borrowed funds is no longer deductible, and if you withdraw from the retirement plan it's taxable income.

Whether you borrow or withdraw, both parties will usually want a formal note, stipulating the terms (amount withdrawn, pay-back schedule, etc.) to avoid confusion.

If you are far-sighted enough to prepare your leave several years in advance and you are fortunate enough to be working for a company that contributes matching funds to your profit-sharing plan, try to get as much out of this account as you can. The idea is to build up as much of your getaway account as possible out of *their* corporate pockets—and then tap this account when you leave.

Another source of funding is your pension plan, providing there is a vested, accumulated cash value. Said Lichtenfeld: "Here, the down side is that there are limitations on what you can actually get your hands on prior to retirement."

You may not think of your insurance policy as a wellspring of cash, but it's one of the best and easiest resources to dip into (short of rich relatives, something we will address later). You may be able to borrow up to the full cash value of your whole life (not term) insurance policy, at rates as low as five to six percent.

Liquidating your assets. If you have stocks and bonds that you're able to sell, take any profit or capital gains in the year that you take your sabbatical. However, if you feel you may incur losses, the benefits from taking them in the year that you return may exceed the benefits of getting your hands on the cash right now. For example, our income was down in the year we took our sabbatical, so we were able to take advantage of that and sell a couple of our retailing stocks for a tidy profit. Our tax exposure was much less because our income was much less.

When trying to plot the great escape, don't look only at the obvious cash sources. "Examine your entire lifestyle," said Lichtenfeld. "Do you really need the second car? Does the motorboat spend more time in the garage than in the water? Is the stamp collection just collecting dust? When looking at your basket of assets, don't overlook antiques, silver, art, jewelry, first-edition books, old records, and even baseball cards."

Joanne Lynch, 46, a divorced realtor with four grown children, examined her lifestyle and sold everything—including her house—to raise the necessary cash for a year-long trip to Europe. "At precisely the time that my peers are concerned with building security, I'm throwing caution to the wind. It seems frightening, but in the end it's very easy. You sell your house and you go. It also helps to have very supportive kids, who understand that my need for a challenge overrides my need for security." (If you are planning on selling your home to finance your escape, get a copy of the IRS's Publication 523, "Tax Information on Selling Your Home.")

Second mortgages. The advantage is that second mortgages are relatively easy to obtain for virtually any purpose. But refinancing can be like robbing Peter to pay Paul: So much of the cash will go to making the mortgage payments while you're away that you'll scarcely come out ahead. An exception, however, is if you already have a lot of equity built up in your home, and rent from your tenant (which we'll talk about in Chapter 5) covers the cost of your new monthly payments. Home-equity loans are another financial tool that's frequently being mentioned these days. According to realtors, the only difference between the two is that a home-equity loan does not require an appraisal; a second mortgage does.

Friends and relatives. Didn't you say that you were willing to do just about anything to get away from the office? Does that include humbling yourself before friends and relatives? They may certainly be more concerned with your happiness than some cold lending institution will be. Of course, whether or not that concern can be converted into cash is another matter.

"Most new businesses are not financed by banks or professional investors, but by family and friends," Lichtenfeld said. "An unbelievable amount of money comes out of the woodwork and there's no reason why that can't hold true for a leave."

HOW TO SPEND
(IF YOU'RE GOING ABROAD)

Saving the money is only half the battle. It's also essential to have access to your funds—no small feat if you're far from home. Carrying bags of money is only advisable if your escape vehicle is a Brink's truck. Checks are out, except in special circumstances. (If you've ever been thwarted trying to cash an out-of-town check, wait until you attempt to cash an out-of-country check.)

Nothing is more frustrating than having money and not being able to use it—except maybe not having money at all. Here are the options:

Traveler's checks.

The undisputed safest way to carry money is in traveler's checks. American Express charges a one percent fee (of the face value of the check), and you do not need an account to purchase them. When purchasing Visa or MasterCard traveler's checks, some banks dispense with the fee altogether for account holders.

Either way, you get the security of knowing that if they are lost or stolen, they can be traced through the code numbers printed on each check. You should keep a list of these numbers and which ones you've spent and you should carry this record separately from your checks. Replacing missing checks without such information is possible, but involves much more red tape. The disadvantages to traveler's checks—albeit a minor one—is that if you are overseas and your checks are not in U.S. dollars, you will have to pay a $2 to $3 conversion fee to exchange them for local currency. (These have a nasty way of adding up. During the course of our trip, we paid $85 in conversion fees.) You can circumvent this by getting your checks in the currency of the countries you'll be visiting, which locks in your exchange rate— a wise move if the dollar drops, riskier if the dollar climbs— which is exactly what it was doing in 1985, when we were traveling. Buying checks in a particular currency makes more sense if you're staying in one place, rather than traveling around. (Save any receipts from exchange transactions abroad; you may need them in order to change the local currency back into U.S. dollars.)

Credit cards.

The second lesson in accessability is to have credit cards. There are American Express offices from Alaska to Zimbabwe and you can draw up to $1,000 with a personal check and a flash of the appropriate plastic.

Borrowing through your credit cards is expensive and should

only be used when in dire straits. In Illinois, where I live, Visa and MasterCard average a whopping 19.8 percent interest. Don't restrict your hunt to the boundaries of your own state. For example, Simmons First National Bank in Pine Bluff, Arkansas, offers Visa at 10½ percent.* (The best card rates are generally offered by smaller institutions; the biggest banks derive much of their profit from credit.)

Cardholders are entitled to other credit card benefits, as well. Diner's Club provides cash advances and free currency exchange at Citibank branches. If you're a Visa card carrier, you can tap into the automatic-teller machines in numerous foreign countries to get up to $200 in local currency. American Express lets you use your local office as your mailing address. (More about mail under "Loose Ends.")

Such convenience means that your money can continue earning interest in your checking account back home. Of course, you'll want to make sure that your checking account offers ready reserve, where the bank will automatically cover any overdrafts (any interest that you may be asked to pay is worth the added security). It means that you don't have to haul around thousands of dollars in traveler's checks (which only earn interest for you know who) or cash (never a wise idea). It also helps to keep the cash flow flowing. We were home for six months before we got billed on some European expenses. One precaution: Check the expiration dates on your credit cards before you leave.

As for disadvantages, there is the ever-present temptation to spend more than you have. And then there are the bills.

Paying bills. There are a variety of ways to handle your debts while you are away. If you are on the move, the most expedient way is to authorize someone at home to write checks in your absence. This can be your property manager (more about that in "Hearth and Home"), a trusted friend, or a relative.

Once you've designated a person to handle your financial affairs, there are still decisions to be made. Should you open a

*As of July, 1987.

separate account solely for that purpose? Or should you write a check to the bill-payer, who will then deposit it and cover your obligations out of his own account? There's no disadvantage to either, but we opted for the second method.

The issue of bill-paying is obviously more crucial for people with no permanent address. If you're going to be putting down roots for three months or more, you might feel more comfortable handling your financial affairs yourself. Opening a checking account in your new location and having your mail forwarded from home is probably the best way to go.

Opening a new bank account. If you're going to be in one place for a while, finding a bank you like and trust is a primary concern. Of course, if you're moving anywhere in the United States, opening a new bank account is simple. If your destination is overseas, it gets a little trickier, but certainly not impossible. *Someone* must be opening all those Swiss bank accounts.

According to Lichtenfeld, the most expedient way is to have a certified check available for deposit at the new bank. As an alternative, the original bank can handle the opening of a new account through traditional banking channels by wiring money ahead. As for letters of credit, he rejected the idea on the grounds that it would be too expensive and unnecessary.

"Every bank with an international department has personnel whose role it is to provide advice for those involved with international transactions, including these. The problem is getting your banker's cooperation and attention when all it involves is opening a checking account or transferring funds. But persistence pays off."

Why not wait until you arrive in town? "It just greases the wheels a little more, rather than coming into a new city from Small Town, U.S.A., where they've never heard of you or your bank."

The wheels will turn even faster if your home bank has a foreign branch in your new location. Several years earlier, on another trip, we lucked out. Cash was running low and we had three days remaining on a cruise. During a stop in Caracas,

Venezuela, we saw a familiar "First National Bank of Chicago" sign, where we made a beeline to the teller's window and cashed a check.

Banks that have foreign branches in the most remote corners of the earth include:

Barclays's Bank International Limited
Manufacturers Hanover Trust Co.
Chemical Bank
Citibank
Bankers Trust Co.
Bank of America
The First National Bank of Boston
The First National Bank of Chicago
Continental Bank
Wells Fargo Bank
Security Pacific National Bank (of San Francisco)

"By planning ahead, the money will be there, waiting for you upon your arrival and it will be 'good' money, meaning that you don't have to wait for it to clear the bank back home," he said.

But don't be so organized that you buy your francs, peso, pounds, or yen ahead of time. "The best safeguard against wildly fluctuating currency is to keep your dollars as long as you can. Except for a token amount ($25-$50) in local currency to get you through the airport and to your destination, there's no reason to purchase foreign currency in the U.S."

As for other ways to minimize losses, Lichtenfeld said there's no easy answer. "The exchange rate plagues big corporations as much as it does you. There's no way to beat it—and if you're going to be worrying about it, you shouldn't be going."

Up to now, the focus has been on where you're going. But no discussion of money matters would be complete without stressing the importance of a good relationship with the bank back home. Several travelers cited examples where the bank covered overdrafts to keep checks from bouncing all over town. Keep your bank informed of your plans and it can be on the alert for any problems.

WILL MY EMPLOYER
GIVE ME HALF-PAY?

You've emptied your basket of assets and turned up nothing but lint. Bankers, friends, and relatives all give you a different version of "Don't call us, we'll call you." It is time to take your pitch elsewhere—primarily to your employer.

Asking your boss to hold your desk open is one thing; asking him or her to help subsidize your getaway is another. The people who ask don't have their hands out, as much as their confidence up. One New Orleans woman who left a sales position with an insurance company to volunteer at a local suicide hot line said that after her leave was approved, she just took a deep breath, looked her boss straight in the eye, and asked about going to half-salary. The worst thing he could say was no. (He did.)

John Feinstein, sports writer for the *Washington Post* and author of *A Season on the Brink: A Year with Bob Knight and the Indiana Hoosiers,* had better luck. He was placed on half-salary during the six months he spent observing Knight's program. The *Post* got Feinstein's weekly column and a story on an occasional game in the Midwest. Feinstein got a best seller.

Most career experts agree that, unless the company has a paid leave policy, having your leave subsidized by the company is going to be a very tough sell. You really have to be able to show that you are going to be conducting company business and that the investment will yield some kind of dividends.

Some companies, like IBM, Xerox, and Control Data, recognize that having employees involved in public service generates good will for the firm and is deserving of some compensation. Others offer stipends to employees returning to school.

If your firm resists the idea of reduced salary, perhaps you can negotiate to keep some of your benefits, such as health insurance. Beginning in 1987, if you terminate your employment, your employer is required to continue regular health coverage up to three years for you and your dependents if you pay your regular premium. Small firms are less likely to offer half-pay but more able to extend a loan, to be paid off (or handled like a payroll deduction) when you return.

"It's important to know your company's policies. Whatever approach you take, there won't be a lot of precedence set, which can work to your advantage," said Nella Barkley of the John C. Crytal Job Center in New York. "So much depends on the size of the firm, what you're doing with your time off and the relationship you have, but it's logical to think that something can be worked out."

A word of caution: If paid sabbaticals are not the norm for your company, then receiving a paycheck—even an anemic one— may also intrude on your freedom. The way Sharon Murrel could arrange to spend 1986 in Belgium was to work for her employer, Bell Laboratories. "While it's nice to get the salary, it would have been nicer to have the time," Murrel said. "I would have studied Dutch and learned to raise orchids. There's so much expertise over here and it's difficult to try and squeeze everything into your spare time. Just think about what you have to give up before you readily agree to work."

THE JOYS OF
(SOMEBODY ELSE'S) MONEY

If you've struck out with the boss, who tells you that you have given new meaning to the word "chutzpah," there is another stop on the money tour: grants, fellowships, and scholarships. Each year, America's 2,900 public and private funding institutions give away more than $3 billion to nonprofit organizations and individuals who have a good idea and know how to sell it.

If you have another *Death of a Salesman* stirring within you, but can't write while you're covering six states selling linoleum, the National Endowment for the Arts—and a $12,500 playwright's fellowship—could get those typewriter keys flying. If studying archaeology in Egypt for a year sounds infinitely more pleasing than a chartered tour of the pyramids, a $5,000 check from the Archaeological Institute of America is a powerful incentive to renew your passport.

Most people assume that grants only go to Nobel Prize winners who are researching a cure for cancer or bringing peace to the Middle East. Nothing could be further from the truth. The Wonder Woman Foundation provides $25,000 to ten women who want "to fulfill a fantasy and represent the qualities and characteristics of the fictional heroine Wonder Woman" (i.e., peace-loving, honest, courageous, compassionate, and wise). That description could fit half the female population of the United States.

So much for stuffy organizations and unachievable qualifications. If you prefer carpentry to comics, then the Haystack Mountain School in Deer Isle, Maine, which is dedicated to teaching crafts to artisans and novices alike, may be your best source of support. But if you are fascinated by humor in painting, you may have to go a little further—like Bulgaria, where the House of Humor and Satire bestows a grand prize of 1,500 leva to some worthy recipient each year.

Competition and eligibility requirements vary greatly. Last year, 7,000 applicants vied for Clairol's Career Advancement Scholarship, which assists women in finishing their college education. The only criteria are that applicants be 30 years old and within two years of completing a degree program. Competition was much less intense at the Slavic Society, which had only five contenders for a $2,000 award for the best screenplay. In Lithuanian.

Elizabeth Hale, a Chicago-based architect, was only 25 when she got a $2,000 grant to attend the Ecole des Beaux Arts in Paris. She had no more grandiose plans than to have a "mailing address" while she explored the continent. "I just applied. I had some good recommendations and used some firm connections and all I knew was that each month, a check would magically come in the mail. I think I just came along with the right application at the right time. I wish I could offer some magic formula, but I can't. I just think I was very lucky."

Whether you're making a pitch to the Ford Foundation or the local Rotary chapter, the advice is the same: do your homework.

One grants administrator after another related stories of haphazard proposals that do not come close to meeting a foundation's criteria. A serious proposal takes time, energy, and self-assessment, so don't leave it for the last minute. An application that is whipped out the night before the deadline is quickly spotted—and eliminated.

The first step is to get a copy of a grants catalog, such as the "Annual Register of Grants Support" or "The Foundation Directory," published by the Foundation Center, an independent, nonprofit organization that offers assistance in locating grants. (See bibliography; you will also find a list of foundations in the appendix.)

Once you have identified several potential sources, contact them for more information, an application form, and a list of recent grant winners. Under the Freedom of Information Act, you can even see a copy of a winning application.

"Establish connections," Hale said. "This is an area where personal contacts count enormously. Find out who is making the decisions and what type of person has won in the past—then go out and make yourself fit the prototype."

There is a knack to playing the grants game, and some perennial applicants have cracked it. Don't be afraid to pump former winners for details, for the key buzz words (like "world peace" used by every beauty contest winner from the Minnesota Pork Queen to Miss Universe). When I applied for the University of Michigan Fellowships, a past recipient confided that one of the judges was an absolute fool for anything that involved World War II. I took great pains to weave the Normandy Invasion into my proposal. I still didn't get the fellowship, but I appreciated the tip.

INTERNSHIPS

Not the answer for someone who wants to lounge in the Lazy-Boy with a bag of Doritos and a beer, but an often-overlooked avenue for people who are tired of their job and have a Walter Mitty desire to try something else.

That was certainly the case with Jeff Meyer, a Seattle stockbroker, who had been active in theater during college. Fifteen years later, the bright lights still beckoned, so he applied for an internship at a London theater.

"It was like getting to go back and spend time with your first girlfriend," said Meyer, whose internship was in technical production. "For four months, I traded a suit and tie for blue jeans and a work shirt. It was great—even though I knew that I would eventually turn back into a pumpkin. Maybe that's why it was so great. If this were permanent, I'd have to worry about some long-term concerns—like supporting myself."

For the short term, Meyer kept the wolf from his door with savings and a stipend of $55 a week. Even without a stipend— which is a far more common internship arrangement—making ends meet is easier for interns than for international travelers. Many internships can be done right in your own home town— and even if you do leave home, there is usually some assistance offered with lodging. So while you may not have any income, you don't have the same outgo, either.

Most interns agreed that money is secondary to love. Since internships can be arranged for relatively short periods, it doesn't take a huge nest egg as much as some judicious budgeting to make it a reality. Tell a rock-music lover that he's going to be reporting to work at *Rolling Stone,* a history buff that there's a slot open in the archives department at the Smithsonian, or a conservationist that Sierra Club needs someone to work on a national environmental campaign, and I can guarantee that the first question won't be about salary.

An added bonus is that internships have the potential of blossoming into full-time employment, making it very attractive for people thinking about a career change. It certainly worked for Steven Spielberg, who started hanging out at Universal Studios in his late teens.

But aren't you a little old to be a "go-fer"? Many people assume—incorrectly—that internships are restricted to students and that the work they will be doing is menial at best. Never have sponsors been so receptive to older and more experienced individuals, or more willing to include them in the day-to-day operations. Indeed, there are many government agencies that *only* accept experienced applicants for internships.

"This is partially due to an increased acceptance to the concept of lifelong learning and partially because an employer would rather get a more mature participant, who already has a degree and work experience behind him," said Mary Lynn Rector, director of the International Human Resources Institute in Boston, which arranges international internships. (Getting foreign jobs and internships is discussed under "Can I Work Somewhere Else?".)

Tips:

• If you are serious about an internship, an invaluable resource is *1986 Internships* (see bibliography), which lists some 35,000 opportunities both here and abroad.

• Don't feel that you're limited to employers who already have formal internship programs in place. If you're hot to work for a particular person or institution, let them know. Ruth Elaine Hanson, a Minneapolis homemaker and superior seamstress, had a burning desire to work for Koos van den Akker, a haute couture designer. She wrote him repeatedly until he eventually acquiesed. She left her husband and two teen-agers and spent the summer in New York, working on the next season's collection. When she left, he gave her one of his trademark patchwork jackets (which now retails somewhere in the four digits) and a job offer, which she declined. "I didn't need to take the job," Hanson said. "What counted was knowing that I was good enough to be taken seriously."

• Don't limit yourself to the most glamorous institutions. While the Metropolitan Museum of Art would be a plum for anyone interested in art history, its internship program is very competitive, receiving some 200 applications each year for 14 spots. The La Jolla (California) Museum of Contemporary Art, on the other hand, received a mere 20 applications for seven positions. Remember, the idea is to break out of your rut and exercise new parts of your brain, not add another feather to your cap.

• If you are free enough to make a two-year commitment, several participants spoke glowingly about a YMCA "World Service Worker" program. Most assignments are in physical education and recreation. All expenses (including transportation and a stipend) are provided. For more information, write:

Overseas Personnel Programs
YMCA of the USA
101 N. Wacker
Chicago, Ill. 60606

GETTING CREATIVE

When no distinguished institution comes forward to finance your sabbatical, that doesn't necessarily mean it goes back in mothballs. You just have to be more creative in your sales pitch, said Matthew Lesko, a Washington, D.C.-based consultant who matches clients with available funding.

"If your fantasy is to fish all summer, then write summer camps and offer your services in exchange for room, board and a small salary," said Lesko, author of *Getting Yours: The Complete Guide to Government Money.* "If you want to play tennis, offer to teach the finer points of a powerful backhand to the handicapped. If you are good at public speaking, the federal government has a program that lets you travel to a foreign country at Uncle Sam's expense, in exchange for extolling the virtues of American enterprise. If you lost a scholarship to return to school, then apply to be a housemother in a sorority house. You just have to look at the problem from every conceivable angle and persevere."

The government program Lesko is referring to is called AmPart (for American Participant) and it is one of the government's main vehicles for fostering effective discussion on major issues with overseas audiences.

Speakers have ranged from Coretta Scott King to the Boston Celtics' Larry Bird, but it has included plenty of "just folks" as well. Speakers who are qualified in economics, politics, literature and the arts, sports, science, and technology are in the most demand. (Foreign language fluency is always desirable, but not re-

quired.) If you feel that you have expertise in a subject that would
be of interest to foreign citizens, contact:

U.S. Information Agency
Office of Program Coordination and Development
P/D, Room 550
301 4th St. S.W.
Washington, D.C. 20547

While traveling at government expense sounds like the ultimate junket my award for the most luxurious way to spend a leave
goes to the cruise lines, such as Cunard, and Royal Cruise. All
offer free passage to men over 50 who have natty wardrobes, do
a mean bossa nova, and are interested in being "escorts." Women
always outnumber men on board, so many ships hire a few escorts
to help balance the ratio and generally be attentive to female
passengers.

If that sounds like a job description for a lounge lizard, Cunard
assures that it's all quite above board. Escort duties include being
available for bridge, dinner, and conversation; to light a cigarette
or pull out a deck chair. Any escort who is tempted to provide any
additional services would do well to consider the consequences: a
heave-ho at the next port. For an application, write:

Royal Cruise Lines
Suite 660, 1 Maritime Plaza
San Francisco, Calif. 94111

Cunard Lines
555 Fifth Ave.
New York, N.Y. 10017

If you possess more stamina than social graces, consider crew-
ing on a yacht. Owners generally provide room and board in
exchange for routine tasks, such as cooking and cleaning. A good
place to begin is with local yacht clubs, which are found in the
yellow pages of the phone book.

CAN I WORK SOMEWHERE ELSE?

Swapping one job for another may strike you as blatantly violating the spirit of a sabbatical. Or it may strike you as a nifty way to pick up some knowledge, not to mention a couple bucks. This is where you go back and review your list of objectives, because that will lead you to two different types of work.

Obviously, the business executive who wants to escape to the French Riviera for nothing more taxing than contemplating the Mediterranean has very different needs than the business executive who wants to learn more about international trade.

If your goal is to get as far away from anything remotely resembling an office as possible and you would work merely as a last resort, then you would be a candidate for unskilled labor, where transients are welcome. In the United States, that's easily done through the "Help Wanted" section of the local newspaper. It is launching a job search abroad that calls for inside knowledge, marketable skills, language proficiency, and lots of luck.

There are dozens of books that go into great detail on the subject of foreign employment, but if you can afford only one, make it *Work, Study, Travel Abroad* by the Council on International Educational Exchange (see bibliography). This unassuming paperback is updated annually and offers endless possibilities— from grape picking in the Rhone Valley to teaching English in Japan. In addition, the CIEE can help you cut through miles of red tape with their "Work Abroad" program. For details, write:

CIEE
205 E. 42nd St.
New York, N.Y. 10017

It is not my intent to duplicate their efforts, but just to hit on some of the highlights. Since each country has different regulations regarding visas and work permits, taxes, etc., you will want to contact the appropriate embassy or national tourist office. With those disclaimers in place, here are some general guidelines:

FOREIGN JOBS

Unskilled. Most countries are just trying to cope with their own unemployment and have no desire to help wayward Americans find a job, but if you don't mind menial labor—either for ridiculously low wages or room and board—service jobs abound, from housekeeping in Holland to harvesting grapes in Greece. It's also an outstanding way to meet people from all over the world. (We returned from Israel with thirty-six rolls of film and an address book fat with names.)

Many refugees from the fast track find menial work a welcome reprieve from the demands of their profession. Said Lynne Miller, who works for a dress manufacturer in New York, about her time as a cook in a Swiss resort: "Chopping carrots for soup while classical music played on the radio was about as far away from the garment district as one can get."

Service jobs—especially during the summer months—can be found all over Europe, Scandinavia, and Australia, although it's more difficult for a Westerner to land something in the Orient. If you're under 30 (although that age limit is often stretched), the United States Travel Service (USSTS) offers a well-organized job program, with the emphasis heavily on agricultural, hotel, and domestic employment. For a $75 program fee, the USSTS will place you in a job according to your abilities, language skills, and itinerary. Many placements are for six to twelve months; a minimum stay of three months is available during the summer only. In addition, the USSTS can secure work permits and provide travel services. For more information, write for the "Working Abroad" pamphlet (see appendix).

Another highly regarded program is International Work Camps, sponsored by Volunteers for Peace. Jobs (in exchange for room and board) range from construction to social work, agricultural to architectural, according to Peter Coldwell, the executive director.

"Work stints last anywhere between two weeks and one month and you can move from one site to the next, so there is a great deal of flexibility," said Coldwell. "At each site, the composition of volunteers changes, so you have a completely different experience. This is the only program that is mutually funded by the East and the West, so it provides a unique opportunity to reach across the Iron Curtain and promote international understanding, good will, and peace." To peruse the variety of jobs and locations, write for the *International Workcamp Directory* available in mid-April for a $6 tax-deductible contribution (see p. 206).

Another option is volunteering on a kibbutz or other farm collective, a terrific way to meet people from all over the world. Most require a minimum one-month commitment (there is no maximum), and experiences can vary greatly depending on the size, affluence, and friendliness of the kibbutz. Not all jobs are agricultural. Volunteers are always needed for kitchen, laundry, and childcare duties. In addition, many kibbutzim have their own factories, manufacturing everything from contact lenses to plywood. For more information, contact:

The Israel Government Tourist Office
350 Fifth Ave.
New York, N.Y. 10001

Archaeology is a field that carries an aura of glamour, although anyone who has ever spent a day digging under a blazing sun will tell you that it's a long way from Indiana Jones. During our leave we saw numerous excavation teams—some required experience, others just required brains and brawn (emphasis on the latter). The Archaeology Institute of America annually publishes a *Fieldwork Opportunities Bulletin*, which lists various excavation sites in the United States, as well as abroad. For a copy, send $6 to:

P.O. Box 1901
Kenmore Station
Boston, Mass. 02215

As romantic as many unskilled jobs may sound, it would be irresponsible to paint an overly rosy picture. Cooking, cleaning, gardening, are hard work and the novelty quickly wears off (although one position I came across—an apprentice jockey on an English stud farm—sounded intriguing).

Skilled. If you're considering a "real" job overseas, remember one word: contacts. They can be found everywhere—from Fortune 500 companies with foreign branches to ethnic associations, from your university to your professional association.

According to Mary Lynn Rector: "Most people interested in working abroad don't look hard enough in their own backyards. Sometimes, all it takes to meet the right person is to attend a conference in your field to find out who has operations abroad and who is hiring. The Sunday papers in most big cities have ads for foreign jobs; or just stop at the appropriate embassy and inquire about hiring practices."

There is a growing demand for Americans willing to take on short-term assignments. "As we move more and more towards a global economy, the need for Americans increases. No longer must someone with an interest in international business make a long-term relocation commitment."

Other tips:

• If you are over 40, are interested in a six-month stay, and have some considerable business expertise to offer, investigate the International Executive Service Corps (622 Third Ave., New York, N.Y. 10017). The tradeoff is that your time won't be your own, but you will go in high style. A former Exxon accountant was sent to Nairobi to establish financial controls for a Kenyan pipeline company. His accommodations? The plush Inter-Continental Hotel. Other compensations—such as a paycheck—vary according to the assignment.

• Health care professionals also have an easier time finding foreign employment. When we were in Israel, the kibbutz dentist would change about every three months, thanks to a program that offers American dentists a plane ticket and accommodations in exchange for their services. The best leads can be found in professional journals or with Direct Relief International, which runs a voluntary medical services program that places qualified personnel in the Caribbean, Africa, and the Orient. Write: P.O. Box 30820, Santa Barbara, Calif. 93020.

• Teachers are always in demand overseas—not only for American schools and military bases, but for tutoring foreign students. If you love being in the classroom but would also like to expand your horizons, a foreign teaching assignment may be a perfect fit. Commitments are usually for two years. For more information, write the Department of Education, 400 Maryland Ave., S.W., Washington, D.C. 20024

• Another government-sponsored program is operated by the Department of Defense, which is responsible for the education of army brats overseas. Assignments are for one or two years and applicants must agree to go wherever the Pentagon sends them. Write: Department of Defense, Teacher Recruitment Station, 2461 Eisenhower Ave., Alexandria, Va. 22331.

If you can't be a teacher, you can always be a student. The range of programs that are available is nothing short of astonishing—and could easily fill a separate volume.

An absolute gold mine is called *Transitions Abroad*, a bimonthly magazine devoted to "overseas travel with an educational or work component." A recent issue offered a chance to study music in Munich, Polish in Lublin, and Islamic philosphy in Cairo. A one-year subscription costs $15 and is available by writing: P.O. Box 344, Amherst, Mass.

Space prevents me from saying much more than 1) Thousands of opportunities are out there, and 2) You don't have to be rich. If it's been a while since you've been in school, you probably remember studying abroad as a privilege limited to debutantes and boys who had numerals behind their names. Today, it's a whole new ball game. Skeptics need only visit the international programs office of your local college to be convinced.

A final word. . . . Whatever your interest, let me emphasize the importance of ingenuity. Take your search beyond the kind of formal programs you find in books. Marcia Lewandowski, a Chicago teacher, found her leave in *National Geographic.*

"I was fascinated by a story on an archaeological dig in Mexico, so I wrote and said, 'I'll carry your photo equipment, I'll record data, I'll do anything if you just cover my expenses.' " Two months later, she found herself in the Yucatan studying ancient Mayan culture. I heard similar stories from leave-takers who worked in Rome, dubbing Italian movies into English, and restoring a church in Barcelona.

Said Lewandowski: "I would have to study for years to learn what I did during those seven months in the Yucatan. Be curious, be aggressive, and don't be afraid to act."

The purpose of this list is to give you an idea of the scope of funding that is available and to get you started. It is by no means comprehensive, nor does it deal with such specifics as application deadlines or selection criteria. For more details, consult the directories listed under "Grants, Fellowships, and Other Money Sources" in the bibliography.

DOING IT ON YOUR OWN

No one is handing out fellowships so you can lounge in your backyard hammock, and you don't want to be an intern—in fact, you don't want to do or be anything. The problem with accepting money is that it usually comes with strings attached. What do you do if your dream is so frivolous that no benefactor would even *dream* of being associated with you?

You do it anyways. Said Bolles: "If you think it's someone else's responsibility—your employer, your union, your government—you'll probably stay right where you are. It's a fact that no one is as concerned with your happiness as you. It's up to you to take the bull by the horns and forge ahead."

You cut up your credit cards and start cutting out coupons; you stop going to the movies; you stop giving pricey gifts; you bring conspicuous consumption to a screeching halt. In short, you rise to the challenge of living frugally.

At this point, ask yourself this question: How badly do I want this sabbatical? Because this is where the purse strings draw shut. For us, no expense was immune from the chopping block. Lunch at some white-tablecloth establishment—once the high point of my day—was now replaced by the ubiquitous brown bag. Silk blouses no longer went to the cleaners (at $7 a trip) but to the bathroom sink filled with Woolite and water. A $30 impulse purchase may seem like small potatoes until you realize that (at 1987 exchange rates) $30 buys you one more night in a two-star hotel in Cannes, Amsterdam, or Venice.

So how much do you need? Once again, that depends on where you're going (if at all), for how long, if you'll be working, what type of accommodations you'll have (a discussion on lodging can be found under "Hearth and Home") and the style in which you like to travel. Your two variables are always a delicate balance of length of trip versus lifestyle. Fond as I am of splurges (to me, "roughing it" was a black-and-white TV), we indulged in three good restaurants in eight months. First, such economy measures never felt like deprivation, since it was so easy to replace the restaurant void with other sensory pleasures. (One of our fondest memories is listening to street musicians in Avignon, while feasting on freshly-baked bread and cheese for less than the price of a Big Mac.) Second, when penny-pinching means adding another city to your itinerary, it is a powerful incentive to bite the bullet. (See "Five Ways to Save" below.)

FIVE WAYS TO SAVE

Americans are notoriously poor savers. Last year, they kept less than 4 percent of their after-tax earnings, compared to 20 percent for the Japanese. If money has a way of flying out of your hands, here are some tips to help your getaway account grow.

• *Make savings a habit.* Pick a realistic amount that you could save each month and then stick to it. Treat savings like rent, food, or any other monthly expense. Pay special attention to the kind of items that you've always regarded as conveniences (cabs, gourmet take-out), but are, in reality, luxuries. Like dieting, if you cheat here and there, you could easily throw in the towel altogether.

- *Trade debt for equity.* After you pay off an auto loan, for example, write the same monthly installment checks—but make them payable to your savings account.
- *Enlist a savings policeman.* Use all the tricks in the book to keep you on the straight and narrow, including payroll deductions that automatically deposit part of your salary into savings accounts or company credit unions. What you don't see, you don't miss.
- *Keep your investments liquid, safe, and with low fees and transaction costs.* Start simply by seeking a free checking account. Some have no or low minimum balance requirements. Some banks offer NOW accounts (Negotiable Order of Withdrawl) that pay savings account rates. The excess over a certain amount will earn a higher interest rate with all the benefits and conveniences of a checking account.

If you are interested in the stock market, opt for "no-load" mutual funds that are no-load (those free from commission charges). If you must tap that money sooner than you think, you won't have to worry about recouping the commission. For example, The Fidelity Fund family has over fifty funds with different investment focuses and unstructured exchange privileges, all no-load or low-load funds. So, as the market varies, you may wish to switch your funds into an investment with a higher return.

Generally, avoid tax-free investments for two reasons: First, tax rates are being lowered beginning 1987 and over the next three years. Second, your income will be less in the year of your leave. Between these two occurrences, it is unlikely that you'll be able to enjoy the full benefits of a tax-free investment.

- *Shun interest expense like the plague.* It is better to have no interest income and no interest expense than it is to have $1,000 interest income and interest expense. Beginning in 1987, interest income remains taxable while interest expense is only partially (and soon to be not at all) deductible.

When putting a pencil to paper, don't forget to estimate *all* travel expenses. That may sound like stating the obvious, but judging from conversations with others, this is a common mistake. For months, your energy has been so channeled into just getting away that it's easy to gloss over how much money you'll need to get around once you're there and how much you'll need to return home (a good reason to buy a round-trip ticket). If you're traveling by car, camper, or boat, have enough elasticity in your budget to cover a dead battery or a leaky radiator. I've provided several sample budgets on the following pages to cover a variety of sabbaticals taken by escape artists at a variety of income levels. Prices change, currencies fluctuate, but these should give you a basic handle on expenses. Of course, cynics recommend putting your clothes in one pile and and your money in another, then cutting the first pile by half and doubling the second.

The best advice, however, still comes from the Boy Scouts. Be prepared—for anything, including acts of God or government. We know only too well the importance of an emergency fund. One week before we left Israel, the travel tax (payable when departing the country) was suddenly doubled from $150 to $300. While the tax punched some large holes in our budget, we were able to continue our trip, but only because we had built in a safety net. You may never need it, but it's nice to know that it's there.

THE BOTTOM LINE

Here are three sample budgets for three vastly different leaves. No budget can be exhaustive or universal. These are furnished as guidelines for someone contemplating an extended trip.

The cruise and the European trip include occasional splurges. Both have plenty of room to cut back, depending on your tastes and priorities. (For example, entertainment may be an easily trimmed item.) The U.S. tour, on the other hand, is more no-frills. Of course, inflation and fluctuating currencies will also determine how far your dollar will stretch.

No budget is included for someone taking a leave at home because no one knows your regular monthly expenses better than you. Also, highly individual items such as car payments, school debts, etc., have been omitted in an attempt to make this as universal as possible.

ONE-YEAR CRUISE FOR TWO

Route: New England through Virgin Islands to the Windward and Leeward Islands (St. Maarten, St. Bart's, Curacao, Aruba) and back.

Boat registration, customs fees	$64
Clothes, drugstore items	310
Dockage	398
Entertainment	420
Fuel (except stove)	750
Gifts	130
Groceries	2375
Haul-out	253
Fishing licenses	35
Laundry	125
Liquor	490
Marine supplies	555
Medical and dental	295
Medical insurance	590
Photographic supplies	160
Postage, phone calls, publications, etc.	160
Restaurants	325
Shoreside transportation	220
Stove fuel	55
Miscellaneous	365
Total	$8,075

Six Months in Western Europe for Two

Route: England, Netherlands, Germany, Switzerland, Italy, France.

Accommodations* 180 nights: 90 @ $30 per night (cities) 90 @ $20 per night (country)	
	$4,500 (per room)
Transportation**	600
Food (breakfast is included in the cost of most hotels)	2040
Entertainment	400
Gifts	150
Laundry	125
Medical insurance	500
Photographic supplies	100
Postage, phone calls, etc.	80
Miscellaneous	300
Total	$8,795

*Rental of an apartment or cottage, if preferred, would run about $1,000 per month.
**The price of airfare to Europe is not included, since there are dozens of fares available at various times of the year from various U.S. locations.

Three-Month United States Tour for One

Route: Chicago west through the Dakotas, Wyoming, Washington, California, Arizona, New Mexico, Texas, Mississippi, Alabama, Georgia, Florida, the Carolinas, Virginia, New York, New England states, and back to Chicago.

Transportation (car, all paid up)	
Gas/Oil	$750
Food	1,200
Gifts	50
Entertainment	750
Laundry	30
Medical/car insurance	200
Photographic supplies	50
Postage, phone calls, magazines, etc.	50
Miscellaneous	150
Total	$3,230

May 1, 1985

Our time here is rapidly slipping away. I have very mixed emotions about leaving the kibbutz, but I'm also excited about facing new challenges.

I won't miss the laundry, the factory, or the kitchen. This week, I had what is arguably the worst job on the kibbutz: washing 90 frying pans in an acid solution. While I was scrubbing away, I inadvertently touched my mouth. Almost immediately, I felt a burning sensation in my throat, followed by a tingling in my left arm. I was convinced that I was poisoned, but it's now 6 P.M. and I'm still here, so that's a good sign that we should make plans for the weekend.

May 3, 1985

Returned from a weekend of traveling to find a party in progress right outside our apartment.

All our friends were gathered around a fire, eating, drinking, and singing. Walking up the road, I heard Amir's accordian music floating in the distance. I broke out my clarinet, which had been gathering dust since high school. Looking at these faces—from Argentina, Brazil, Chile, Canada, England, and South Africa—I was overwhelmed by how fortunate we were to have seized this opportunity, to take one last look at a time that everyone told me was long over. The only difference is that this time it's even better because I'm savoring it more.

May 7, 1985

Dave worked rounding up the turkeys for market from midnight to 5 A.M. He came home exhausted and filled with contempt for the dumb birds. Manual labor continues to lose its luster.

While he was recovering from his stint, I took the afternoon off and went to Jerusalem. Even five months later, the city is like an onion: There's always another layer to peel back.

Everything we do now has a certain urgency. Even Michael feels transition in the air. Today, he and Niko—who had spent every day since January beating up on each other—hugged each other and sobbed. We've all had longer relationships, but we've never had more intense ones. For five months, we've eaten, slept, worked, and lived with these people. It's going to be very hard to say goodbye.

May 24, 1985

A new travel tax—passed yesterday and effective tomorrow at midnight—has complicated our lives. We will have to pay $300 apiece just to leave the country. That's $900, and that puts a serious dent in our budget. Dave went to Tel Aviv, traipsing from one travel agent to another, but everyone else had the same idea. It's a real panic situation—people pushing and shoving, as if there's a pogrom in the next village. Just when it seemed as if every plane, boat, bus, and camel was sold out, Dave came back clutching three tickets to London. Departure time: 11:30 P.M., exactly 30 minutes before the new travel tax goes into effect.

May 25, 1985

A steady stream of people have been coming by to wish us "bon voyage." (Sergio and Zoila wished us "good sex," which, apparently, is the traditional farewell of Chile.)

As my last day in Israel slips away, my only regrets are sightseeing ones. I never got to the Beduoin market in Beersheva or the artists' colony in Safed—proof that no matter how long you spend somewhere, there's always one more place you want to squeeze in.

Two hours before our departure, Michael had a terrible reaction to bug bites. His entire body was covered with large, raised welts. He looked so pitiful; he couldn't even walk because his feet were so swollen. The kibbutz doctor suggested that we might want to delay our trip, but we decided to go ahead and, if necessary, seek out medical care in London.

Stanley and Rachaeli took us to the airport and we all hugged and tried—unsuccessfully—not to cry. Are we making a mistake by not staying permanently? Will our lives ever be this uncomplicated again?

May 27, 1985

We arrived in London at 4 A.M. this morning and found a nice little hotel near Victoria Station. Michael's swelling has gone down a bit, although walking is still difficult. When he got tired, we returned to the hotel, climbed under the covers, and watched "The Three Stooges" (which he called "The Three Students"). There's a feeling of continuity when your own children laugh at the same things you did thirty years earlier. TV . . . bathtubs . . . magazines. After the kibbutz, life's essentials now seem like luxuries.

May 31, 1985

Sailed from Harwich at midnight for Amsterdam. We staggered off the boat at 6 A.M. and took the train into the city. We were totally unprepared for the beauty of this city.

After we checked into our hotel, we rented a canal bike and pedaled the waterways right up to Anne Frank's front door. This nondescript brick building inspired more reverence from its visitors than many cathedrals and national shrines.

It is the mundane in Anne Frank House that makes such an impact on visitors: spice jars, an ironing board, pictures of Ray Milland, Ginger Rogers, the princesses—Margaret and Elizabeth—tacked to the wall, just as Anne had left them. No one has "spruced up" the house for tourists. Everything was left just as it was when the Gestapo banged on the door forty years ago.

5

Hearth and Home

Pulling the plug on your life takes infinitely more planning than it did back when your most prized possession was a bricks-and-boards bookcase.

Now you may be fueling a lifestyle that includes everything from property taxes to health-club contracts. It's a lifestyle that took more than a few weeks to build and it's going to take more than a few weeks to dismantle. The key is to do it methodically, kicking down one hurdle at a time.

Discussing the mechanics of a sabbatical are not nearly as romantic as perusing travel brochures on Australia. As much as you may want to ride off into the sunset, there are dozens of mundane details that must be arranged. It is tending to these details that can make the difference between a getaway that's an unqualified success and one that's a disaster.

"What makes the planning so difficult is that just when you are most determined to throw off the shackles of civilization, it is the shackles that demand all of your attention," said Mark Ugowski. Ugowski speaks from experience. He sublet his apartment to a tenant who later took off and left Ugowski holding the bag for two months rent.

Finding a tenant is just the beginning. There's insurance to pay, perhaps furniture to store and mail to forward. If you are spending an extended period abroad, you have to make decisions about where your children will go to school and what to do with your pets. You don't realize how complex your life has become until you try to simplify it.

A checklist will be invaluable, not only to keep track of all you have to do but also to remind you of how much you've accomplished. (I've provided a sample at the end of this chapter.) Above all, don't get overwhelmed. There's no mystique to leave-taking, just tenacity, stamina, and ambition—qualities that most fast-trackers have in abundance.

LOOKING FOR MR. GOODRENT

Unless you are lucky enough to find a tenant who is a million-aire in an iron lung, renting your home is an experience that is guaranteed to produce disappointment—eventually.

The first step in what may be an arduous process is to lower your expectations by half. You are simply not going to find a tenant who will care for your home like you. However, there are several precautions you can take to ensure that your home does not look like a two-year-old's playpen upon your return.

Take your time to find a qualified tenant. With all the anxiety involved in subletting, there's a great temptation to take the first candidate who can walk upright through the front door. Be patient. There are a lot of renters out there—especially if you live in a city like New York or San Francisco, where good rentals are hard to find. Assuming that your rent is competitive, you can develop a pool of prospective tenants, from which you can pick and choose.

Have prospective tenants fill out an application form, listing their employers, previous residences, and credit references. This is *your* home—if you are an owner, not a renter yourself, it's probably the single largest investment you will make in a lifetime, so don't be shy about asking personal questions. We called a reference of seemingly impeccable tenants only to have their previous landlord go into a seizure at the mere mention of their names. Apparently, they stripped his apartment of everything—right down to steaming the wallpaper off the walls. Needless to say, we quietly lost their application.

Determine the rent. Research what rents are in your neighborhood. Do not be surprised if you cannot fully cover your monthly principle, interest, taxes, and insurance (PITI). This is a rough economics lesson on why apartment buildings were converted into condominiums faster than you can say "tax break." Mortgages—especially those at 10 to 14 percent (common prior to 1986)—don't lend themselves to low rents. Another hidden fact is that your homeowner's insurance (including personal property coverage) could be half the cost of business rental insurance. While you're accustomed to paying $25 or more a month for your homeowner's insurance, now you've got to start paying $40 or more for business rental insurance. Remember when I told you that nobody is going to take care of your home like you? Well, the insurance company feels the same way, and if you are not living on the premises, expect to pay more in premiums. Again, the only silver linings are tax ones. Even under the new tax laws, insurance is tax deductible when you rent your own primary residence. Property tax and interest on your mortgage are deductible either way. In some states, property taxes may increase if you are not living in the primary residence. However, now you've got rental income to report on your tax returns.

Write a lease. You can buy a standard lease form at most office-supply or stationery stores. However, it's just a tool, so don't be afraid to edit it to fit your needs.

A major point to establish on any lease is the purpose of tenancy. You want to make sure that the people who are renting your home are using it for a residence and not for a wholesale carpet business or SWAT assault practice.

Of course, this is the place to describe the property and specify terms. Are you renting your home furnished or unfurnished? Does the rent include utilities? Use of the car, boat, snowmobile, and bicycle?

Who is responsible for raking the yard or removing the snow? Is parking included? How many and what type of vehicles are allowed on the premises? (Some driveways are not designed to handle semi-trailers.) What about cable TV and ham radios? Are the tenants welcome to use everything—including your grandmother's crystal—or are some things off limits? Be sure to spell out the terms very clearly.

Determine what you will and will not accept. Some people don't mind pets, but loathe children. Or smokers. Or tuba players. Decide what kind of tenant fits your needs and don't panic if you don't find him or her right away. Of course, it never hurts to be flexible. We started out with a no-pets rule, only to break it when a reputable contractor answered our ad. She could patch a roof, unclog our rain gutters, and fix the plumbing, if necessary. She also had not one, but two dogs. We bent the rules and never regretted it.

Spread the word. Where do you find prospective tenants? Running a newspaper ad is an obvious place. (Save your receipt, it's tax deductible.) This is not the time to be modest about your home. If you can offer a superb view, location, or architecture, say so in the ad.

There are other places that can yield excellent results. Consider posting notices at local colleges and universities. Some schools have a housing bureau, where they take rental information over the phone and run it everywhere from the faculty lounge to the alumni newsletter. Short-term rentals are especially attractive on campuses, because of the number of visiting professors who come into town. Once again, be specific. There can be a big difference between renting to freshmen and to graduate students in theology.

Major corporations also play host to visiting executives. Call personnel departments of local companies to advertise your home.

Hospitals are another good place to post your notice, as are law offices, newspapers, magazines, and TV stations. Any place that has a steady stream of interns is a potential gold mine for renters. (Another option—house swapping—will be discussed later in this chapter.)

Finally, many people have located tenants by relying on word of mouth. Tell everyone you know of your search. It could be that the best friend of your neighbor's brother is searching for a place for only six months—a match made in heaven.

Hire an accountant and an attorney. Many people regard this as an extraneous step, but if it gives you extra peace of mind it is well worth the expense. Our accountant helped us spot some tax-deductible items that we otherwise would have overlooked. Our attorney gave us a couple of good tips on warranting the working order of our appliances, which we incorporated into our lease. Most of us rest easier knowing we have a document that will stand up in court if it has to. God forbid.

Appoint a property manager. You've found a renter and collected a month's damage deposit. Now you have to sort out the logistics: How is the tenant going to pay your rent, and how do you know it's being paid and the checks aren't bouncing and the water heater is still working?

You need someone to represent your interests and to make sure that money is being deposited and that the property is being maintained. Some people ask a friend to perform this vital function, but nothing will strain a friendship faster than a call about a broken furnace at 3 A.M. in January. This is no place for an amateur. Skimp somewhere else, but hire a professional property management service or someone who owns rental property and doesn't mind adding one more address to the list. The latter is what worked for us. In exchange, we paid our property manager the equivalent of one month's rent. It was worth every penny. (It's also tax deductible.)

This person should also be given power of attorney while you're gone—expressly and solely for the purpose of renting your

home in the event that something happens with your tenants—
something bad. We had one tenant who got a sudden job offer—
2,000 miles due west. Our property manager placed an ad and had
new tenants without so much as losing a single day's rent. We
weren't even aware of the problem until after it had been solved—
a great source of relief, especially if you're on the other side of the
world.

Make sure that your property manager is able to deposit the
rent checks in your checking account, and make sure that your
mortgage, insurance, and property taxes are directly deducted
from this same account. Notify your bank of the changes, so that
monthly statements can be forwarded to your property manager's
address. Also make sure that your property manager (or someone
else you designate) has the power to be the co-signer for any
accounts related to the maintenance of the property and payment
of bills. Notify your bank of any changes, so that monthly statements can be forwarded to your property manager's address.

Get out the magnifying glass. Inspect your home with your new
tenant, noting nicks, dents, and scratches. This saves a lot of
trouble when you return. ("That gaping hole in the wall? That was
here when I moved in.") Take the time to inventory and photograph your belongings. This not only serves as a record of their
condition, but their existence.

Said Judith Specht, who swapped her Malibu home for a London address: "To let strangers come into your home, you have to
start out with a basic trust in people. If you're going to worry,
don't do it. I just left my things out—and everything was pretty
much the way I left it."

Prepare a "how-to" book on your home. A manual on your home
can be an invaluable resource to your tenants. This is the place to
include everything that makes your house tick: garbage pickup,
location of the fuse box, names and numbers of repairmen and
exterminators, how to operate everything from the Cuisinart to
the fireplace. (Most gas companies have year-long maintenance
insurance, available at a nominal fee, similar to automobile ex-

tended warranty programs. For an up-front premium, they will provide labor on all your gas appliances, which saves you from falling prey to some fly-by-night operator.) Any helpful information will be appreciated by your tenant. One leave-taker even traced the outline of every key, so there would be no question as to which one opened the door, the garage, and the mailbox.

Also worth including are any tips on the neighborhood: best carry-out Chinese restaurant, cleaners, and hardware stores, for example. We kept a loose-leaf notebook on the kitchen table in the months before we left and recorded items as they occurred to us.

Finally, it's a nice touch to introduce your new tenants to your neighbors. It's good public relations and it will help make the newcomers feel at home.

RENTER RECOMMENDATIONS

If a homeowner sublets his residence and is not prudent in his choice of tenants, the consequences can be financially disastrous. When a renter sublets, his liability rarely exceeds his damage deposit. Still, the objective is the same: finding an upstanding citizen who will adhere to the terms of the lease.

Some tips to help subleasing go smoother:

1. Make sure that you are allowed by the terms of your lease to sublet your apartment or house.
2. Inform your landlord of any subletting arrangements. Discuss how the payment of rent should be handled.
3. Inspect your apartment thoroughly with your sublessee, documenting any spots on the rug, burns on the counter, etc. It takes a short time and saves a lot of hassles when you return.
4. Discuss the security deposit with your tenant and let him know that he will be responsible for any damage to you, but that it's up to you—not the landlord—to collect. It's your name that's on the lease.
5. Arrange for the payment of electric and telephone bills. (Translation: Take all billings out of your name.)

6. Leave a forwarding address with your sublessee and with the management office of your building.

7. Inform your sublessee of procedures regarding parking, security, garbage, laundry rooms, etc.

Don't be put off by all these warnings. I've tried to alert you to the worst-possible-case scenarios. While there is no shortage of catastrophic sublet stories, there are as many that are really successes. While we've had tenants who left teeth marks in the furniture, we've had more people who left the place in better shape than when they moved in. Just check those references—and keep your fingers crossed.

SHORT-TIMERS

Finding a tenant is not something you can wrap up in a weekend. Is it worth going through all these gyrations for a shorter leave, say three months or less?

That's a question that depends completely on your personal circumstances. If finances are tight, even one month's rent coming in from a tenant may be crucial.

When weighing the pros and cons of a sublet, don't only look at the monthly income from your tenant. Also consider the costs (such as advertising) you'll incur locating your tenant and accommodating him (such as storing your own stuff). But if your best friend's sister is moving to the city, doesn't own a stick of furniture, and needs a place to live, you won't have to spend a cent. That's why each situation must be evaluated on its own merits.

CAR CARE

Storing your car is another detail that isn't nearly as exciting to think about as the temperature in Tahiti; but it is important, especially if you want to have transportation when you return.

For short getaways (less than six months), the best solution is to find a trusted friend who will dutifully start the engine every week or so. Longer absences (six months or more) calls for a more complex regimen, according to Bob Sikorsky, who writes a nationally syndicated column on cars and is an automotive consultant. While rendering a car inoperable is an undeniable hassle, it does carry some insurance benefits. If your car cannot be driven—even by thieves—then suspend your liability insurance, retaining only the comprehensive coverage. The savings can be in the hundreds of dollars. But don't be tempted to drop all car insurance. If a fire, flood, or tornado hits, the premiums will look like a bargain.

Now for Sikorsky's no-fail formula for long-term storage:

1. A car is always better-off stored inside, preferably in a cool, dark, and dry environment. The temperature should never drop below freezing.

2. Remove the battery.

3. Drain the fuel system. Any gasoline left in the bottom of the tank after draining should be siphoned out.

After the tank is drained, the engine should be run until all the gas in the lines, carburetor, fuel pump, injectors, and other system parts is used up. If the car uses leaded gas, run with a gallon or so of unleaded before draining and drying the system. Unleaded gas left in the fuel system is less likely to form deposits when it evaporates.

4. Change the oil and filter as close as possible to your date of departure. Storing a car with old oil will wreak havoc on your engine.

5. Ideally, a can of molydenum disulfied (MoS2) should be added with the oil change. The car should run with the new oil/MoS2 combination for about two hours before the final shutdown. The MoS2 will coat the engine parts and make them almost impervious to moisture.

6. Pull the spark plugs and pour about a teaspoon of fresh engine oil into each cylinder. Then replace the plugs. This helps coat the cylinders with fresh oil.

7. All engine openings should be packed with some type of absorbant cloth.

8. The air-cleaner opening and oil-breather cap should be packed while the engine is warm. The same applies to the exhaust pipe, but wait until it has cooled.

The rest of the engine procedures should be done when the engine is warm. Don't do them on a cold engine because you will be sealing in moisture instead of keeping it out.

Ideally, the engine should be started about once or twice a year and run for at least thirty minutes.

Release the tension on all the drive belts in the engine. Fill up the transmission and rear axle fluids. If your automatic transmission fluid hasn't been changed in the last 30,000 miles, it would be a good idea to get a fresh fill before storage.

Radiator coolant should not be drained. The cooling system should be left wet to help preserve the various seals and gaskets inside. The coolant should be fresh, preferably a permanent type with a rust inhibitor. (Here's an exception to the radiator rule: If any part of your engine is aluminum, then drain the cooling system. Electrolysis set up by the aluminum and coolant combination can corrode and ruin an engine. It's better to replace a few seals than an entire engine.)

Brake systems should also be left wet. If the fluid is old, change it. Over time, old brake fluid will corrode and pit metal brake-system parts.

If the car is to be left for a year or more, put it up on blocks or jack stands. This takes the pressure off the wheel bearings, shock absorbers, and tires.

If the tires are good, they should be removed. Leave them mounted on the wheels with the pressure slightly reduced, and store them on their sides out of the sunlight.

If the car can't be put up on blocks, then add another 10 to 15 pounds of air to the tires.

If the car is stored inside, it is best left uncovered. The interior should be cleaned and vinyl coated with a quality protectant.

If stored outside, a good quality car cover is recommended, and some type of frame should hold it above the car's finish so it won't rub the paint. Cover the interior (dashboard, rear deck, and upholstery) with clean white sheets or towels. Cover all the windows so the sun doesn't penetrate, but leave one window open just a crack.

Whether storage is inside or outside, the car should be washed and waxed, and you should run some type of silicone preservative on all rubber door gaskets and other rubber parts.

Finally, keep a list of all the above steps, and place the list in the car so that you'll know just what you have to do when you return.

STORAGE

The idea of storing the contents of an entire household is enough to make anyone throw up his hands. Fortunately, memory is mercifully short. A few days into your leave and you won't even remember what it was like trying to store a St. Bernard and a grand piano.

Moving all your belongings and then retrieving them upon your return would not only be expensive but wildly impractical. Such a logistical nightmare is what caused us to reject otherwise perfect tenants: a doctor and his wife who had just sold their home and needed a place to rent until they retired to Florida six months later. The problem was that they wanted us to remove all our furniture. Next application, please.

A far more common arrangement is to store selectively. Many people derive great comfort from knowing that their beloved antique desk, record collection, and grandfather clock are under lock and key. The crucial question is can it be replaced? If the answer is no, then start exploring places to store your stuff.

This is the time to cultivate friendships with people who have garages, basements, and attics. If no one fits that description, there are other options—at a price, of course.

Storage lockers are available in many places, in all shapes and sizes—a testimony to our mobile society. Prices vary, but an average national figure (meaning everywhere but Manhattan) for an unheated 5 × 10–foot space is $35 per month. Add 15 percent more for heating, which is preferred if you're storing stereos, computers, musical instruments, or anything else that would be affected by extremes of temperature or humidity.

The savvy storage seeker will look for a clean, secure, and fireproof locker, with a resident manager on the premises. Some storage lockers even offer pickup and delivery—a thoughtful accommodation—as long as the service is not built into the price. If your storage fee includes insurance for the full value of the goods stored, your personal property insurance can be reduced for the period while you are away. Since policies vary—especially regarding periods of suspension—each case must be evaluated by a competent insurance agent.

The flooring in most lockers is merely a concrete slab. Some experts recommend storing your boxes on wooden boards (pallets) or on carpet remnants to keep the contents dry. Condensation is the enemy, whether you're stashing Chaucer or a cello.

"If you're storing an instrument, you'll want to wrap it with a blanket," said a spokesman for Steinway Piano. "Just that simple precaution will do wonders in keeping dust and moisture out. If possible, try and get a locker located in the middle, rather than the ends, which are more exposed to the elements."

Books are another item that require some tender loving care. Books are best packed in boxes, which are then placed—but not sealed—in plastic bags. For best results, alternate the bindings to keep pressure from building up on the books' spines.

Leather-bound volumes should be oiled periodically (good advice even if they're not headed for storage). A $10 kit made for this purpose can be obtained at bookstores that specialize in rare and antique volumes (or write the Newberry Library, 60 West Walton, Chicago, Ill. 60610).

Even if the books stay on the shelves and the piano stays in the parlor, every landlord must empty closets for the tenant. The fringe benefit here is similar to spring cleaning: You are forced to purge your wardrobe of mistakes dating back to 1967.

Every piece of our clothing needed to be mercilessly scrutinized and acted upon. Clothing fell into three categories: packed for the trip, packed for thrift shops or other charities (don't forget the tax-deduction form), or packed for the cleaners (which meant asking the hard question: "Do I *really* want to pay $5 to keep those bell-bottoms?"). Every cleaner has a different policy, but we paid $25 a season (over and above the cost of the cleaning) to store our clothes. Not only was it a terrific bargain, but it was a terrific psychological boon to come home and find our entire wardrobes clean, pressed, and bagged.

Finally, consider a safety deposit box for your valuables. If you already own a box, you may want to bump up a size to accommodate family silver, jewelry, or other heirlooms. Banks will gladly upgrade your box, but don't wait until the last minute; it's not uncommon to find a shortage of just the size you want.

Possessions take time, energy, and, above all, money to store, protect, move, and clean. After you get a few estimates for storage, you'll be surprised at how easy it is to sweep away the sentimentality. Here are some suggestions on clearing out the clutter:

- Don't hang on to something just because it was expensive. If your purchase was a mistake, cut your losses and get rid of it. Hauling a box of junk over to your neighborhood consignment shop not only gets it out of the house but can put some cash back in your pocket.

- Don't procrastinate. If you've been saying for the last five years that the wing chair will look terrific once it gets reupholstered—and the chair is still sitting in the garage—the chances of it happening are remote. Sell it and recoup some of your investment.

- The same is true for clothes. If you haven't worn it in two years, get it out of your closet.

- Peruse magazines for articles you want to keep. After spending an entire Saturday in a damp basement, going through a five-year pile of back issues, I will never again save an entire magazine for a raspberry soufflé recipe that I will never make.

- Don't hold on to every school paper your child brings home. Sentiment is fine—within reason.

- The same is true for souvenirs. After all, you've got to make room for all the new stuff you're going to collect during your adventure.

TAKING CARE OF PETS

What do you do with a dog or a cat? No one can deny that
many people consider their pets beloved members of the family.
A recent University of Maryland study showed that 36 percent of
the survey respondents "viewed their pets as people, while another
8 percent saw them as falling somewhere between an animal and
a person."

But no matter how many human qualities we seek to endow
our pets, foreign countries and airlines are not quite as whimsical.
Bringing Fido along on your leave is not impossible, but it certainly will add a few headaches to your getaway.

The biggest hurdle is that most countries require long periods
of quarantine. For example, in Great Britain, dogs must be quar-
antined for six months and you pick up the tab for the boarding
expenses. In addition, your pet may face another isolation period
when you return to the United States.

A far easier solution is to board Fido at home. The most
economical solution is to find an animal-loving friend who will
take this responsibility seriously. If that excludes everyone you
know, there are numerous facilities that will take any pet for any
length of time, and prices are more reasonable than you'd expect,
especially when weighed against the expenses of transporting and
caring for your dog abroad.

One highly recommended company, American Pet Motels,
Inc., is based in Chicago, with a list of new motels under construction that rivals Sheraton's (Houston, Dallas, Los Angeles, and
Washington, D.C. are slated for 1987). In addition to kennels and
catteries, the company maintains an aquarium, serpentarium,
bunny club, and simian salon, in case you need a place to keep
your chimp. At this "Plaza" of the pet set, Fido's accommodations will probably be more upscale than yours, including FM
music, air conditioning, wall-to-wall carpeting in every room,
afternoon cookie breaks, and round-the-clock medical care.

"We pride ourselves on taking care of a pet's individual
needs," said Robert Leeds, company president. "Right now, we

have a parrot who won't eat unless he gets to watch his afternoon game shows, so we found him an eight-inch TV. It's only black and white, but it seems to have done the trick."

Rates at most pet boarding facilities start at $7 per day (more if your pet demands a suite); however, long-term discounts are available. While your pet can probably live without TV, there are certain niceties that are standard for every guest, such as heating and an indoor/outdoor running area. In addition, a reputable facility will require proof of vaccinations and will look well-maintained. "Never board your pet where you're not allowed to examine the premises," said Leeds. "That's a sure sign that something isn't quite right."

Perhaps the costs—both financial and emotional—are too prohibitive to leave your pet behind. Transporting your pet is possible, but if you are going overseas, know the regulations before you get to the airport because they are rigidly enforced.

While there are some variances from country to country, be prepared to furnish a certificate of good health (signed by a licensed veterinarian sometime within the last seven days) and a rabies vaccination at least 30 days old and not more than 180 days old. As an added precaution, ask your veterinarian to look up the diseases and parasites native to your destination to determine if any additional shots should be administered. The foreign consulate will be able to give you detailed information on entry requirements, which may include a veterinarian certificate endorsed by the Inspector of Charge, Bureau of Animal Husbandry, U.S. Department of Agriculture, and an import license.

Other tips:

• Airline regulations are as restrictive as customs. If you are flying with your pet—either domestically or internationally—know that most airlines will not accept any animal for shipment if the temperature is below 40 degrees or above 80 degrees Farenheit. Dogs and cats should wear a flea-and-tick collar and identification tags. The pet's leash should be removed and attached to the cage, where baggage handlers can get at it, if necessary. Also attach a cloth bag of food (enough for the length of the flight) and a tag with your overseas address and phone number.

• If your pet is elderly, high-strung, or has a history of motion sickness, you may want to ask your veterinarian to administer a tranquilizer prior to departure.

• These booklets can help plan your pet's trip:

Touring with Towser (a directory of U.S. hotels and motels that accommodate guests with dogs, $1.50 check or money order)
Gaines Kennel Directory
P.O. Box 8177
Kanakakee, Ill. 60902

Traveling with Your Pet ($4 check or money order)
ASPCA Education Dept.
441 East 92nd St.
New York, N.Y. 10128

INSURANCE

Insurance is one of those necessary evils. It's not just the fact that it costs money. Plane tickets, backpacks, and hotels cost money too, but somehow I didn't resent those purchases. With insurance, however, you're paying for something you hope you'll never use.

The most essential insurance is medical. To use an insurance cliché, nobody plans to have an accident. Medical costs today are so prohibitive that hospitalization without insurance can be a disaster that could take a lifetime to pay off.

It is this type of emergency that leave-takers fear most. For that reason, it doesn't make sense to pay for a lot of coverage that you find in a standard policy—coverage you won't use, such as office visits and prescriptions. In most cases, you'll want only major medical and hospitalization. While the deductible is high ($1,500–$2,000), it will protect you from financial ruin.

If your employer is feeling magnanimous, your company may

be willing to pick up your health-care benefits; but don't hold your breath. According to a spokesman for Charles D. Spencer & Associates, which publishes employee benefit information, quality family coverage can cost anywhere from $2,500 to $4,000 a year. It is the rare employer who wants to absorb that kind of bill if you're not there wiping the sweat off your brow.

Here are the options:

• Convert your group plan to an individual plan.

According to Amy Biderman of the Health Care Insurance Association of America, this would be impractical for most people because the costs would be prohibitive to everyone but oil barons. "About the only reason someone would make this choice is if they had a pre-existing medical condition (hypertension, diabetes, emphysema, etc.) which would make them very difficult to insure."

• Continue paying your group rates.

For most people, this is the optimum solution, since rates for group insurance can be half of what they are for an individual. If, for some reason, you do not wish to follow this option, you may qualify as part of another group outside of your company, such as fraternal organizations, alumni groups, churches and synagogues, or even credit-card holders.

• Get an interim policy.

Many companies—such as Blue Cross/Blue Shield, Travelers, Prudential—have interim policies, which offer major medical and hospitalization at a lower rate. The disadvantage here is that they are rarely available for periods longer than sixty days.

• Go without insurance.

This is terribly risky, but single people who are young and healthy may be willing to dispense with insurance altogether. If you're tempted to play the percentages, don't do so without earmarking about $2,000 for medical emergencies, which will cover an emergency room visit, X-rays, laboratory work, and even a follow-up visit. Put it aside in a separate account, where, we hope you'll never need it. The worst-possible-case scenario is that you'll have something set aside in case a disaster strikes; the best is that you'll have a tidy nest egg when you return.

FINDING A PLACE TO LIVE

Since your largest expenditure—about 40 percent—goes to putting a roof over your head, it is the price of accommodations that cause most people to throw up their hands and downscale their plans.

This is another place where fortitude, perseverence, and ingenuity will serve you well. Remember no pain, no gain? Looking for long-term housing isn't painful, it's just that most people don't have the faintest idea of where to look.

One thing is certain: Unless you're very wealthy, you can't pull up in front of a swanky hotel. Except for the occasional splurge, most U.S. hotels are too costly over the long haul. Even a no-frills motel goes for $25 a night—and that's half the national average.

So you've picked up some books on student travel—and decided that you're a little too old for sleeping at the train station. (One book actually recommended getting arrested as a way of securing lodging. You may not need room service and a color TV, but you shouldn't have to figure bail money into your budget.) There are ways to get more for your money.

Judith Specht and her husband traveled to England for five weeks last summer with their daughter and her girlfriend. They stayed in a converted villa and even had a car at their disposal. The cost? Absolutely nothing.

Home swapping. The Spechts swapped the use of their own home and car in Malibu, California. They are among a growing number of Americans who are stretching their travel dollar through home-exchange clubs. For $15, the Spechts could list their home and their preferred destination in a club directory— and then wait to see who bites. Obviously, their Malibu address gave them an edge over someone from, say, South Dakota, but according to David Ostroff, there's a potential match out there for everyone. (In 1983, Colorado Governor Richard Lamm exchanged the official governor's mansion for a San Francisco townhouse. This was not a big hit with the legislature, which pointed out to him that the mansion was not his to swap.)

Home swapping has a surprisingly high success rate. In addition to the obvious financial benefits, there is the added convenience of having someone to water the plants, feed the dog, and take in the mail.

"Maybe one out of twenty home exchanges are failures and five out of every twenty are absolutely super," Ostroff said. "The rest are in the general success category. The best matches are usually the ones where there is good planning and good communication established between the participants."

The club's subscription forms give people a chance to evaluate the exchanges. "Disappointments usually occur over differences in housekeeping standards. One person's definition of 'clean' may not be the same as yours."

Indeed. While Judith Specht took pains to plant a garden and leave a bottle of champagne in the refrigerator ("I felt as if we were representing the United States"), her swap-mate left accommodations that "had not seen a vacuum cleaner in years."

While the Spechts' experience was not without its glitches—including finding out that in London a "converted villa" means a boarding house and being surprised by several hundred dollars in long-distance calls on the phone bill when they returned home—would she do it again?

"Absolutely," she said, without a moment's hesitation. "But I would do things a little differently." She offers the following suggestions:

• Research the location of the house you are considering. That way you won't be surprised when "near the beach" turns out to be three miles instead of three blocks.
• Ask for photographs of the interior of the home and a complete description of the facilities.
• If you are concerned about the telephone, disconnect it.

For more information, contact the following organizations:

Vacation Exchange Club
12006 111th Ave.
Youngstown, Ariz. 85363

(Listings are $16; directories come out in February and April.)

Loan-A-Home
#2 Park Ave.
Mt. Vernon, N.Y. 10552

($35 for an annual subscription; $30 for one directory.)

Inter-Service Home Exchange
Box 87
Glen Echo, Md. 20812

(Membership fee is $24, which covers your listing, receipt of twice-yearly catalogs, and a booklet of guidelines for exchanges.)

Global Home Exchange and Travel Service
P.O. Box 2015
South Burlington, Vt. 05401

(More than a simple listing, this agency has firsthand knowledge of both the accommodations and their owners. For a $250 fee, the staff checks out every detail and makes the necessary arrangements. However, they only operate in England, France, Germany, and Switzerland in Europe and the East and West Coasts in the U.S.)

Home and apartment rentals. If you wanted to rent a beach house on Nantucket for the summer, you'd check with realtors in the area or the listings in local papers; but where do you start house-hunting if the house you want is a Swiss chalet or an Italian villa?

Your best bet is to start with the U.S. branch of that country's national tourist office. (Most are in New York, but some also have branches in Chicago and Los Angeles.) Many tourist offices will naturally want to steer you towards home rental organizations, which, in turn, will want to steer you towards pricey accommodations. Be patient. After being told that most London properties rent for $1,000 a month, one friend ended up in a very pleasant flat in the desirable Kensington neighborhood for about $600. One of the most complete listings of national tourist offices, as well as rental agencies, can be found in "Travel Basics" (see bibliography).

Camping. If you're a novice, this isn't recommended for an extended period, but camping has its devotees and does offer the kind of challenge that some leave-takers are seeking. It certainly can't be beat for traveling on the cheap. A Golden Eagle passport ($10) offers free admission to most national parks, forest recreational areas, and other public lands. Campsite rates vary, but rarely top $10 per day. Not every park accepts reservations, but they can be made at the most popular sites, such as the Grand Canyon.

For more information, write:

The National Park Service
Box 37127
Washington, D.C. 20013-7127
202-343-4747

On campus. Dormitories, fraternities, and sororities are filling a need for both travelers looking for ways to cut lodging expenses and colleges looking for ways to earn revenue during the slow summer months. Some 300 colleges and universities now offer rooms for as low as $10 per night. Besides the savings, many offer great locations—like Stanford University and northern California's wine country, Northwestern University and Lake Michigan, Tulane University and Bourbon Street and the Fashion Institute of Technology and all of Manhattan. Some throw in kitchen privileges and the use of recreational facilities—such as swimming pools, running tracks, and tennis courts. For more information, contact the housing office at the school you want to visit.

Bed and Breakfasts. The days when the Widow Jones would rent an extra room with a four-poster bed, charming Laura Ashley prints, hand-made quilts, and fresh caramel rolls in the morning for a mere pittancc are pretty much history. The general public has discovered B&Bs and the prices have risen accordingly. Throughout the country, daily rates of $65 and up are not uncommon; but if you're willing to get off the beaten track—especially in the southern United States—you can still find some bargains ($15–$25) and stay in some beautiful historic homes to boot.

Generally, the rooms in privates houses with shared baths are less than country inns with private baths and brandy at bedtime. If you have any doubt that this quaint way to travel has become as mainstream as a Holiday Inn, look at the travel section of your nearest bookstore, where there are at least two dozen books on the subject. One of the best is *A Treasury of Bed & Breakfast,* which lists 3,000 homes and about 150 reservation services throughout the U.S. and Canada. If you're interested in a B&B abroad, check a guidebook from the country that you're interested in or contact their embassy.

For more domestic information, write:

American Bed & Breakfast Association
Box 23846
Washington, D.C. 20024
202-379-4242

Bed & Breakfasts International
151 Ardmore Rd.
Kensington, Calif. 94707
415-525-4569

A CHECKLIST
FOR THE TRAVELING LEAVE-TAKER

1. Budget your escape. Remember that your biggest expenses come up front (plane tickets, camper, etc.)

2. Sublet your home or apartment (see sample sub-lease agreement on the following page).

Sub-Lease Agreement

I, _____, a Sub-Tenant, hereby agree to

sublet Apartment No. _____at , Any Town, U.S.A. for the

period of _____from _____to _____at a rental

of _____DOLLARS per month, payable in advance on the
first day of each month during the term of Sub-Tenancy hereby
created.

I further agree to surrender the apartment at the end of the term
hereby created in like good order and repair as now is, ordinary
wear and tear and the elements excepted.

I further agree to abide by all the terms of the original lease and
rider executed by and between XYZ INCORPORATED,

and _____, blank copies of which are attached hereto and which
become a specific part of this agreement.

_____
SUB LESSEE

_____
SUB LESSEE

DATE: _____

3. Investigate schools for children (discussed in the next chapter).

4. Start exploring options to board pets, if you have any.

5. Store your car or sell it.

6. Store your personal belongings. If you need a storage locker, leave enough time for comparison shopping.

7. Check on health insurance.

8. Stock up on toiletries; have extra eyeglasses made, if necessary (discussed in the next chapter).

9. Talk to an accountant or an Internal Revenue Service (IRS) agent about your changing tax status.

10. Get a safety deposit box for valuables.

11. Change utilities to the name of your tenant. It's not necessary, but it's highly recommended. That way, if your tenant falls behind in his bills, it is his credit rating that will be affected, not yours.

12. Prepare a book that describes your house: how things work, important numbers, names of repairmen, etc.

13. If you're going on a paid sabbatical, arrange for automatic deposit of your salary check to bank account.

14. Cancel newspaper subscriptions and re-address or suspend other subscriptions.

15. Pack.

16. Alert relatives, friends, and especially neighbors to your departure. They can be that extra pair of eyes while you're away.

June 7, 1985

We planned on spending a couple days in Amsterdam and ended up staying a week. Traveling without an itinerary is so liberating. We can extend our stay or take an unscheduled detour because we don't have to be back at the office Monday morning. I never realized how preoccupied we were with work, even on vacation.

We took the overnight train to Lucerne, Switzerland. Both the train and our seatmates—a Dutch painter and a German stripper—were charming. We went to bed with windmills and woke up to chalets and snow-topped mountains; the entire country looks like a music box.

After the no-frills life of the kibbutz, the conspicuous consumption of Lucerne is overwhelming. Tour buses surround leather boutiques and jewelers like covered wagons circling the Indians.

American students are all over the place and living on even more of a shoestring than we are. I'm sorry that we didn't do this when we were younger.

June 9, 1985

Venice is the one city worthy of the overworked adjective "unique." Everything is just as it should be—the gondolas, even the laundry flapping between buildings.

June 15, 1985

A day not without its tensions. I learned my first lesson in Italian retailing: no returns. After scrimping, saving, and staying at some $20-a-night "toilettes," I blew $40 on a pair of shoes that I didn't want and didn't need. Just fifteen minutes after the trans-

action, I returned to the store and explained that I had changed my mind and would senora be good enough to take back the shoes? What could be simpler? Fifteen minutes earlier, she was explaining the nuances of suede with all the fluency of a product rep; now, she couldn't speak English. I left, defeated. The only silver lining is that Michael instantly came to my rescue. "Mom, would you just take my money?" he asked insistently. Is this the same kid whose opening line is "What did you bring me"? His generosity, genuine and without hesitation, will be a cherished memory—and that's worth 40 bucks any day.

6

Kith and Kin

Dealing with cars, insurance, and storage is the easy stuff compared to friends and families. Numbers are cut and dried, but relationships are rarely that simple.

As euphoric as you are about this adventure, recognize that not everyone is going to share your enthusiasm. In other words get ready to put up your umbrella, because someone is going to rain on your parade.

If you are braced for the inevitable onslaught of naysayers, it will help you keep your steely resolve. Someone (usually a child) will tell you how this is going to ruin her life because she was elected to student council; someone else (usually a co-worker) will tell you how many rungs you'll slide down the corporate ladder; someone else (usually a parent) will call you frivolous, irresponsible, or—dare we say it—selfish. One Dallas mother wasn't even subtle; she pressed the ultimate guilt button when she told her 43-year-old daughter, a lawyer, that "I'll probably die while you're in Europe."

You don't have to go abroad to encounter opposition. Numerous leave-takers related stories about being excited about returning to school, remodeling a basement, or stepping up their volunteer activities only to have well-meaning friends and relatives take the wind out of their sails. And that hurts.

"I was raised with a tradition of community service," said one woman who took a six-month leave from her position in a blue-chip New York law firm to work at a woman's shelter. "I thought my parents would be proud, but instead they acted betrayed."

Stuart Sugarman, head of psychiatry at the University of Connecticut Health Center, said such choices tug at our allegiances.

"We are obligated to be loyal—whether that means to our real families or our employer families; but the cost of that loyalty can mean the sacrifice of one's own selfhood. There comes a point when you realize that loyalty to one's self must be placed above loyalty to others."

But isn't that terribly egocentric? Is it wrong to want that validation for what we are about to do? To want our families and peers on the sidelines cheering us on?

"As one matures, the shift should be away from external approval and towards internal approval," Sugarman said. "If you can approve of yourself, you are in a much better position to meet your needs and to control your own destiny."

Here comes another catch-22: People who are run down are probably in the weakest position to meet their own needs. Just when you need to reach down and pull up as much courage and self-esteem as possible, it's in the shortest supply.

"If you have nothing left, you have nothing to give others. Paradoxically, if you are taking care of yourself, you are better able to give to the people around you and ultimately be a better employee, spouse, child, or parent. People can only be as connected and giving to others as they can be selfish and independent about their own needs."

Sugarman said that a first step towards a successful leave is shaking off the need for approval. "In fact, expect anger and hostility because you are rocking the boat. If you find yourself wavering, it may help to remember that the ability to tolerate the anger of others really means the ability to believe in oneself."

PARENTS

Otherwise articulate people—the ones who have no trouble speaking before the board of directors or a filled-to-capacity banquet hall—find themselves tongue-tied when it comes to talking with their parents. If you can barely manage telling your folks that you're breaking tradition and spending Thanksgiving in Aculpulco, how are you ever going to tell them that you're leaving a good job?

If you have parents who are vigorous risk-takers and urge you "to go for it," consider yourself lucky and skip the next few pages. But most parents need to hear about your plans very gently. Coward that I am, I broke the news in a letter. This gave me an opportunity to control the conversation and explain our decision in a calm, rational manner—something that never could have happened if I had delivered the news verbally.

Since parents of those in their 30s and 40s came of age during the Depression, the thought of leaving any job—especially a good one—is anathema to everything they stand for. To the previous generation, "I worked forty years for the railroad" brought instant respect and admiration. Indeed, the measure of a man's maturity was how few changes he made in the course of a lifetime—one spouse, one address, one job, and one gold watch upon retirement. Today, few people have any intention of spending their entire career in one place.

In all probability, your life is already vastly different from your parents', whether it's working while you still have young children, taking a vacation with a friend (instead of a spouse), or seeking therapy. If you take the time to explain why you need this sabbatical and that it is not something you've done capriciously, they almost always come around. (My own parents went from total disapproval to making their first overseas trip to visit us on the kibbutz, a remarkable leap of faith.)

Some parents respond less favorably to their childrens' independence than others, said Jean Prebis, associate professor of psychology and gerentology coordinator at Purdue University.

"They usually fall into two camps—either the martyr (remember the "I'll probably die when you're in Europe" line?) or the dictator ("You're throwing out your career. How could you do something so stupid?"). Assume your parents won't change and the only behavior you can modify is your own. Nobody can make you feel guilty unless you give them the power to do so. In short, you can flatly refuse to be a victim," Prebis said.

"I don't think relationships change that much as you get older. The point at which you leave home is pretty much where your relationship stays. Over the years, you may keep up the appearance that everything is terrific; you may relate through the grand-children or manage brief periods of interaction, like Christmas and birthdays, but your relationship never progresses beyond the point it was when you left the house. The same unresolved conflicts just simmer below the surface."

What if your parents don't simmer, but boil over with indignation at your decision?

"The first step is to tell yourself that you refuse to be bullied. The next step is to tell your parents 'Mom and Dad, I dearly love you, but we are going to take this sabbatical and we will write and we will call and you'll come visit us and we'll bring you back a great present. I'm sorry you're unhappy, but we're still going to go ahead with our plans.' When you take one step, then it becomes easier to take another and another. Rarely is the way in which family members relate to each other changed in one fell swoop, but rather you chip away at it, one behavior at a time."

"It really has to do with taking control, and that's not something you can do unless you really believe in yourself," said Arnie Zipursky.

"Our parents didn't agree that this was the best use of our money. They would have preferred to see us use the $15,000 we spent traveling as a down payment on a house. We knew what they thought, but we also knew, in our hearts, what was right for us. There would be time later on for houses and children, but there may not be time for this kind of leisurely travel. While their objections are motivated out of love, their needs are different than ours. Things like security and a financial cushion are more important to people in their 60s than for people in their late 20s."

However, there is a difference between leaving parents with doubts about your priorities and leaving them with genuine health problems. No matter how certain you are of your decision, if your parents are elderly and/or in poor health, their welfare will weigh very heavily on your mind. (Of course, this concern is not limited to leave-takers, but to all people who are more than a few time zones away from their parents.)

The decision to stay or go has a lot to do with the current role you are playing in your parents' health care, said Prebis.

"Too often, adult children feel that they're the only ones who can look after Mom and Dad, and the parents may reinforce this idea very strongly by whatever they say or don't say. Consequently, their children's lives are in limbo."

As part of her gerentology practice, Prebis sees many adult children who have made elaborate plans and now must put them aside.

"Obviously, it's very frustrating. How you evaluate where you are now is measured against where you thought you were going to be. To be care-giving at a time when you thought you'd be getting some time for yourself is disappointing. It has nothing to do with love, it's just not what you had planned. Then you feel guilt on top of your disappointment, which only makes the situation doubly stressful."

The crucial question is how do you balance the needs of both the care-giver and the care-receiver?

For the chronically ill, Prebis said that temporary arrangements with a nursing home can be made. "This is the solution for many people who go on vacation. Obviously, it is of utmost importance to explain that this is a temporary situation. Other options can include having a care-giver come in to the home; or, if there is some self-sufficiency, having a neighbor check in periodically. Talk with your parent and your parent's physician to determine which is best."

Leaving phone numbers where you can be reached isn't a problem if you're going to be renting a beach house for the summer or going back to school. But if you're constantly on the move, keeping in touch with the folks back home is considerably tougher. I devised a system that gave me and my parents some peace of mind as we were traveling through Europe. Each time we came to a city and located accommodations, I checked in at the American Express office and left our local number. When we left a city, I would leave word of our next destination. Even though we could not be pinned down to a strict itinerary, they had a vague idea of the countries we were visiting and in which order. If ever there was an emergency back home, we were leaving a trail so we could be located. It was a lot cheaper than long-distance phone calls.

SCHOOLS

What to do about your child's schooling has a lot to do with your own definition of education. There are parents who want their children in a structured school format, as similar as possible to the one they left. Other parents opt to take their children out of school, using travel as an education in itself.

First, can parents legally take their children out of school? Trying to find an answer to this question is like trying to catch smoke—with a net. Requirements vary from state to state, but regardless of where you live, the very first step should be your school principal. Some school districts give their blessing and others treat it as truancy. A lot may depend on what kind of alternative arrangements you have made.

For those constantly on the move, an accredited correspondence course may be the arrangement of choice. Despite the image of a school advertised on a matchbook cover ("Draw this dog"), many correspondence schools have excellent academic records. If you would like to check on a school's accreditation, write the Office on Educational Credit and Credentials of the American Council of Education, 1 DuPont Circle, Washington, D.C. 20036.

While it's true that a correspondent student won't be able to try out for the football team or cheerleading, most of the other aspects of school life—such as geometry homework—transcend the miles.

For elementary school children, the best-known program is the Calvert School in Baltimore, founded in 1897 and approved by the Maryland Department of Education. Calvert's curriculum covers the basics (reading, spelling, arithmetic, history, etc.) as well as the humanities (mythology, poetry, art history). Transcripts of grades and teacher evaluations are transferred, so children don't miss a beat.

As of 1986, tuition ranged from $135 (per year) for a kindergarten course to $385 for grades 7 and 8. Along with books and lesson plans, tuition includes supplies—right down to crayons and erasers. For more information, write:

Calvert School
105 Tuscany Rd.
Baltimore, Md. 21210

There are more options for high school students. Two of the best known include the University of Nebraska's Continuing Studies Program and the American School. Both have impeccable and established (starting in 1929 and 1902, respectively) reputations. Studies show that their students rate very favorably (SAT scores, college performance, etc.) when compared to "permanent" students. (College-bound seniors are eligible for scholarships as well.) An average semester for a freshman (algebra, English, social studies, and a foreign language) would cost about $250 a semester at American, or $35 a credit hour at Nebraska.

"We have a diverse student body," said Nancy McKeown, principal at the American School. "It has included entertainers like the Osmonds and athletes like Andrea Yeager, but it has also included children of business executives and an 88-year-old widow, who looked forward to her lessons as a way of coping with loneliness. Students are all over the world."

For more information about their programs, write:

American School
850 East 58th St.
Chicago, Ill. 60637

University of Nebraska, Lincoln
Division of Continuing Studies
269 Nebraska Center for Continuing Education
Lincoln, Neb. 68583

For families who are staying abroad in one location, a more formal academic situation is recommended. Even then, your decisions are just beginning. Do you want your child to attend an American or a local school? A local school offers a richer and more diverse experience, but it can also require a long and painful socialization process. Only you know your child and know which situation will yield the best results.

For more exhaustive information on schools available overseas, write the cultural affairs officer at the American embassy in your new location or The Office of Overseas Schools, Department of State, Washington, D.C. 20520.

American International Schools cover kindergarten through 12th grade, are located in forty countries, and are so accustomed to transient students (children of diplomats, business executives, professors) that tuition is pro-rated by the month. The curriculum and grading system are the same, and credits do transfer once you return home.

Other options include U.S. military schools (open to nonmilitary dependents, providing they are American citizens) and English-speaking private schools. Tuition and academic standards vary, but many—such as the institutions run by the Anglican Church—have excellent reputations. For more information, contact the embassy of the country you'll be visiting (generally, brochures are available, which describe the school system in detail) or *Schools Abroad of Interest to Americans* (Boston: Porter, Sargeant), which is updated annually.

The parents and students I interviewed were overwhelmingly positive about their children's school experiences abroad. Invariably, parents cite the more serious approach to studies, the international student body, and an emphasis on manners as fringe benefits of their sabbaticals. "All of a sudden, my kids started using 'sir' and 'ma'am' when addressing adults," said one mother, who had her two teen-agers in a Geneva, Switzerland, high school.

"After years of interpreting one grunt as 'yes' and two grunts as 'no,' it was sheer heaven. . . . In the suburban high schools, different is bad; everyone wants to talk, dress, and act like a clone. But abroad, *everyone* is different, so you don't have the same peer pressure. They were free to be themselves and I think that, more than anything else, gave them a confidence that would have been hard to find at home."

How can you ensure that your experience is as positive?

"Try and choose a school where student mobility is common, not where your child is going to be the first, the second, or even the tenth new kid," said Fran Goldenberg, who teaches fourth grade at a public school located near the University of Chicago campus. Over the years, she has seen numerous children—including many from overseas—transfer in and out, as their parents temporarily relocate for graduate school, fellowships, and other academic pursuits. "It just helps to have a teacher who is more in tune with the needs of a new student," said Goldenberg, who always teams up a new child with a "buddy."

She also recommends that if you are going to a foreign country, you try to teach your children even a few words in their new language beforehand. And if the entire family enrolls in Berlitz, that's wonderful, but not necessary.

"Parents should relax about their children's language skills, because the kids pick it up much quicker than the adults," Goldenberg said. "I recently had a student in my fourth-grade class from Finland who could not speak a single word of English in September. By the time school was out, he was reading English at a fifth-grade level. Many of the kids who transfer in belong to families where there are books in the home and there is already an emphasis on learning. Once you're literate in one language, it's not difficult to become literate in another."

Whether you're going to spend a semester in Paris, France or Paris, Texas, there are some steps parents can take to help their children fit into a new school system:

• If possible, time your arrival to coincide with the new school year.

• Take a "dry run" before the first day of school—everything from where to wait for the bus to a look at the classroom. It will make the whole procedure more familiar and less threatening.

• Find out if your school offers any special orientation programs for new students.

Perhaps the most important lesson is to remember that a leave should not be viewed as a solution to family problems. If there *are* problems, being thrown together in a London apartment for six months is not going to make everything okay. In fact, it will probably make things worse. But if a child is doing well at home both academically and socially, chances are good that he'll do well somewhere else, and this will be a rich and rewarding experience for the entire family.

OUTSIDE THE CLASSROOM

There are some excellent books available on traveling with children. While I don't want to duplicate their efforts or dispense mundane advice (does any parent need to be told how to play "Let's see how many different license plates we can spot"?) there are a few hints that we picked up along the way that are applicable, whether you're traveling for one week or one year:

• Resist the urge to cram culture, architectural landmarks, and breathtaking scenery down your children's throats. Don't be upset if your child prefers an Archie comic book to the Grand Canyon or if Michaelangelo's David brings hoots and giggles. Even the best-behaved children can take only so much culture before they literally start climbing the walls. We had a great deal of success alternating one child activity with one adult activity. While we saw twelve zoos in Europe (many of which would not qualify as pet stores back home) it was a small price to pay for family peace. One benefit: By seeking out city parks and playgrounds, we met a lot more local folks than we would have ever met at the Hilton.

• Praise positive behavior. The time for a lecture is when your child does something right.

• Anticipate as many problems as possible. If a fight breaks out over who gets to sit next to the window every time you get in the car, devise some system—even drawing straws—ahead of time.

• Take along a tape recorder. Our primary purpose for investing in one was to send tapes home, keeping friends and family abreast of our itinerary. But a fringe benefit was that it was a terrific diversion for long train and car trips.

• Be realistic. No matter how many coloring books we brought along, our five-year-old would not sit through an evening at the opera. However, parenting doesn't mean neglecting your interests entirely; it just means making some judicious choices.

One of our most successful outings—and fondest memories— was seeing *42nd Street* in London, because before we even walked up to the box office we increased the odds in our favor. We went to a matinee (when we knew Michael would be well-rested), we chose a musical with lots of glitzy costume and set changes (this was not the time for *Death of a Salesman*), and we sat in the front row, where the whole extravaganza seemed larger than life. Finally, we bought half-price tickets an hour before curtain—for about $10 a seat. We were willing to gamble $30, but not $60. When you travel with children, never make an investment in entertainment so huge that you can't walk away from it.

• For more tips, write to:

Dorothy Jordan
Travel with Your Children (TWYCH)
80 8th Ave.
New York, N.Y. 10011
212-206-0688

June 20, 1985

We're booked on the midnight sleeper from Rome to Nice. What a surprise to find out that the train was nothing like the one we took from Amsterdam to Switzerland. German trains have many more amenities than Italian ones—like sheets. Here, each passenger is given a yard of gauze to sleep on. It more closely resembles a Stay-Free maxi-pad than anything you would put on a bed.

Our accommodations, however, were nothing compared to our roommates. I dragged our suitcases down the narrow hallway, only to find a 6-foot, 5-inch block filling the doorway of our compartment. He looked menacing—black leather sleeveless jacket over a fishnet shirt and the de rigueur chains. In ten hours, he never once removed his sunglasses or uttered a single word. He slept on his briefcase; Dave slept on his wallet. At dawn, passports were checked at the border. As he unchained and unlocked his briefcase, I craned my neck to catch a glimpse of its contents. It was crammed with pornography and an assortment of firearms. So much for elegant train travel.

June 22, 1985

The French Riviera deserves—and defies—every description. Is water supposed to be such a vibrant turquoise? Are bodies supposed to be so lean and cars so long?

Less than a half-hour after we arrived in Cannes, we were appropriately oiled and slumped into beach chairs—full participants in lifestyles of the rich and famous. (Where else can you see advertisements for "starter yachts"?)

July 2, 1985

Cannes made me think of the film festival, which made me wonder who is going to be the new movie critic at the paper. As all this shuffling is going on, I'm curious about whose stock is up, whose is down, and where I'm going to fit in. I can't worry about it. To be here and let the office intrude is to undo all the benefits of the last six months.

July 29, 1985

We're wending our way towards Paris. In less than a week, we'll be flying back to the United States.

This last leg of the trip is different. Dave talked to his boss and made an appointment for when we return. Already the end is in sight.

I'm anxious to see friends and family. With all the hijackings recently, everyone has been real worried about us and it will feel so good to be together. It's just that we planned for so long and now it's almost over. There's a part of me that just doesn't want to let go.

August 4, 1985

I'm sitting next to a businessman, who opened his briefcase before the plane was even airborne—and then worked virtually nonstop until we landed at Kennedy. God help me if I ever fall back into such habits. No one on their deathbed ever says, "Gee, I wish I'd spent more time at the office."

7

Loose Ends

You've completed every project at work and your "pending" file is uncharacteristically empty. You've got the house rented, the money stashed, and the car stored. But just when you feel smug about your superb organizational skills, a loose end dangles out of nowhere to trip you up. Before you roll out of the driveway, here are some odds and ends that you won't want to overlook.

PACKING IT IN

Now that you've dealt with everything and everyone you're going to leave behind, it's time to discuss what you'll be taking.

You've heard it before, but it bears repeating: Pack light. The convenience of having a particular shirt is not nearly as great as the inconvenience of having to lug around too many suitcases. I speak from experience. After leaving Israel, we were so weighed down by nine suitcases that we had to check half our luggage in London just so we could continue our trip. The offending baggage spent two months in a locker at Victoria Station—at the rate of 50 cents per bag per day—until we picked it up before returning home.

There is a certain freedom that comes from traveling light. As one who is used to traveling with a hair dryer, curling iron, and hot rollers, I threw caution to the wind and left it all behind. I discovered that I could survive very nicely without all the paraphernalia and that there is life without styling mousse. It's a simplification that carried over once I returned home.

Obviously, packing clothes for an extended leave will be a bigger job than for a vacation, especially if you'll be around for a change of seasons. Even so, no one ever seems to return from a trip lamenting that they didn't pack enough.

HEALTH

It's far more difficult to have prescriptions filled overseas. If you're on any special medication, be sure to take enough with you to cover the length of your stay. Make sure all your prescriptions are kept in their original bottles, and if you are traveling with anything that customs agents may find suspicious (like insulin syringes) carry a letter from your physician.

While you're at the drugstore, stock up on over-the-counter drugs and toiletries, as well, if you're going abroad. The virtues of traveling light will be discussed later in this chapter, but this is the one place where you can bend the rules and stock up. Obviously, if your destination is London or Vienna, provisions are less crucial than if it's a Third World country. But even in the most civilized cities, you don't find the mega-discount stores we take for granted in the United States. A few months before D-Day, we started stockpiling shampoo, toothpaste, and other staples until we accumulated almost enough to open a branch of our own. But it was a wise move that looked even wiser after a few months in Israel, where inflation bloated the cost of a tube of toothpaste to the equivalent of $5.

Money is not the only motivator. Sometimes, it's next to impossible to communicate a very specific need in a foreign language. One fellow kibbutznik could not, despite her respectable command of Hebrew, describe the wetting solution for soft contact lenses to a Jerusalem pharmacist; so she ended up having some mailed from Detroit—at ten times the cost.

If you have an infant, you may also want to bring an adequate supply of formula (or find out the name of a comparable brand overseas). Disposable diapers are available in most countries.

If you are going to be staying in one spot, get referrals from your home doctor and dentist. If an emergency arises, the U.S. embassy will provide a list of physicians. The embassy does not rate their qualifications, but does assure you of their ability to communicate in English.

Get an extra pair of eyeglasses made, in case yours are broken while you're traveling.

If you have a serious allergy or health problem, consider purchasing a Medic-Alert bracelet or necklace. Not only can the identification tags be inscribed in any language, but the organization also maintains a twenty-four-hour central registry that will furnish additional health information to medical personnel anywhere in the world. For more information, contact Medic-Alert at 840 North Lake Shore Dr., Chicago, Ill. 60611.

The International Association for Medical Assistance to Travelers (IAMAT) was established to provide a source of medical assistance for people traveling abroad. There is no charge for membership, but donations are appreciated. Membership includes a membership card (which entitles you to IAMAT services at fixed rates), a world immunization chart (which lists immunization recommendations for more than 200 countries), and a physician directory for 125 countries (including those who speak English and received their medical training in the U.S.). To join, write IAMAT, 736 Center St., Lewiston, N.Y. 14092.

Other emergency options include the Medical Passport, a pocket-sized personal health record that is used by the State Department for its overseas personnel and includes a medical family history. It is available to non-government employees by contacting the Medical Passport Foundation, P.O. Box 820, Deland, Fla. 32720 (904-734-0639).

The American Red Cross has a good first-aid kit that can literally be a lifesaver. It comes in a padded case that won't hurt anyone if it's tossed around the car in an accident and it doubles as a pillow to prop up a victim's head in an emergency. Best of all, the kit is organized in labeled pouches with instructions on how to make use of the contents. Pouches cover everything from cuts and scrapes to severe bleeding. Available for $25 plus shipping and handling. Order from the American Red Cross, P.O. Box D, Haworth, N.J. 07641.

If you choose to assemble your own kit, here are some basics:

Antacid
Antidiarrhea medication
Aspirin
Bandages (gauze) and
  Band-Aids
Calamine lotion
Corn pads
Cough medicine
Dental floss
Ear drops (especially
  for children)

Eye drops
Foot powder
Insect repellent
Motion sickness pills
Mild laxative
Scissors
Sunscreen
Sterile cleanser
  (hydrogen peroxide)
Thermometer
Tweezers

IMMUNIZATIONS

Some countries require particular immunizations before entry. Others merely recommend them. To determine what shots—if any—you'll need, contact your state health board. Health experts cite malaria and hepatitis as the two biggest threats to people traveling in underdeveloped nations.

In some areas, cholera, rabies, and schistosomiasis (a tropical disease that can be contracted by swimming in fresh water) are also potential problems. To be on the safe side, check with your doctor and the local health department.

If your destination requires immunizations, don't wait until the last minute. Not only can some shots not be given at the same time as others, but, if you have an allergic reaction, you want to be close to home.

CHILDREN

While we did a good job anticipating our child's medical needs, we didn't do so well when it came to his recreational needs. Toys, particularly in the Middle East, were both expensive and shoddy. We would have sold our souls to get our hands on just one Transformer, He-Man character, or any other refugee from Saturday morning television. It certainly would have come in handy—especially around 6:30 A.M. (parents and children have vastly different definitions of "sleeping in"). There is, of course, the ever-present concern with packing light, but if you value solitude over an extra sweater, pack some new toys and books—to be brought out at that precise moment when infanticide seems imminent.

MAIL

No matter how much you may want to leave civilization behind, that wish rarely includes mail. There was no more welcome sight than letters or a *Time* magazine—even three weeks late—peeking out from our mailbox. News from home takes on such importance when you're away that it's worth the trouble to get the mail forwarded.

The most obvious solution is the U.S. post office, which will forward your mail for up to one year within all fifty states and U.S. territories. If you plan to be on the move or travel farther and longer, you must come up with some other solutions.

The most obvious one is to have your tenant sort through all mail and send the important correspondence on to you. A general rule is that anything with less than 17 cents postage should be tossed immediately, unless you truly believe that your Neiman-Marcus catalog will come in handy in Dubrovnik or that you could be a big winner in the Reader's Digest Sweepstakes.

If this is an imposition on your tenant, have the mail redirected to someone who will perform the sift-and-dump function for you.

(We used our property manager, but parents, friends, and secretaries may also be willing.) Then it was packaged and forwarded to us, usually by registered mail.

Another alternative is to use a professional mail-forwarding service. Some will even take phone messages (for a fee) and include them in their weekly packet to you. Charges average about $15 a month.

Some of the best-known include:

Bellevue Avenue Executive Mailboxes
38 Bellevue Ave.
Newport, R.I. 02840

Home Base
EMP.O. Box 226
Long Beach, N.Y. 11561

MCCA, Inc.
P.O. Box 2870
Estes Park, Colo. 80517

TRA
710 West Main St.
Arlington, Tex. 76013

If you're constantly on the move, the ubiquitous American Express office may be the best place to catch up with your correspondence. Most offices will hold your mail for thirty days free of charge, providing you have an American Express card, traveler's checks, or even an airline ticket issued by the company. Instruct correspondents to underline and capitalize your last name and mark the envelope "Client Letter Service" and "Hold for Arrival" (a precaution, just in case the mail beats you to your destination).

While we were traveling without an itinerary after we left Israel, we were certain that we were going to spend a considerable amount of time in Nice. Consequently, we made that the one spot where we had a reservation and deposit. Not only were we assured of accommodations during the busiest time of the year, but we also used it as a mail collection point. What a joy to check in and have the desk clerk hand us a fat envelope of mail.

TELEPHONE

Nothing will make you appreciate American technology more than trying to make a phone call from overseas. Not only is it frustrating and time consuming, but when you finally do reach your party, you frequently can't hear them very well anyway. A friend trying to make a phone call from her room on the third floor of the Cairo Hilton to Washington, D.C. was told by the operator that she would get a better connection if she moved to the lobby. "Or better yet," said the operator, "why don't you just send a telegram?"

Making a call in Israel was always an adventure. Pay phones do not accept coins, but tokens, which would drop through at sixty-second intervals. To make anything but a collect call would require so many tokens that you would need to bring a wheelbarrow to the phone booth.

If you are renting a place abroad and will not inherit a phone, write as far ahead of time as possible to get one installed (a company letterhead may expedite matters). Even so, it will be excruciatingly slow, even in otherwise civilized countries. In Paris, for example, the national joke is that half the city is waiting to get their phone installed, while the other half is waiting for a dial tone.

Other tips:

• Avoid making phone calls from a hotel room. The surcharges can be astronomical, unless you can dial direct from your room. Many countries have a government telecommunications center (usually found at the airport, train station, or post office), where you can save as much as 50 percent.

• Your getaway may be a good time to get a telephone credit card. There is no charge, but you must have a phone (home, office, parents) where calls can be charged to.

8

Reentry (or You Can Go Home Again)

Coming home is a little like the proverbial good news/bad news joke. The good news is that you are refreshed, recharged, invigorated, and clearly not the same person you were when you left.

The bad news is that everyone else is.

Reentry shock is a syndrome that everyone goes through, whether you traveled the world or never left the city. The gears shift, the calendar turns, and—poof—you're back to the daily grind with only your tan as evidence that it ever took place at all.

Nothing will prepare you for the swift loss of freedom. Instantly, you go from making your own decisions to needing three signatures to requisition paper clips. You go from having an abundance of time to no time at all. While we were away, it simply didn't matter when we got up or when we went to sleep. All of a sudden, these things not only mattered, they ruled. Our lives had been free of watches, schedules, calendars, and lists. In the blink of an eye, they reappeared. Gone were the novels and in their place were a flurry of pink "while you were out" notes and yellow "stick-um" notes, reminding us to pick up the cleaning, the groceries, the child. For eight months, our decision-making was of the "do we go to the beach or do we go to the city" variety. Now it was "do we fix the car or do we fix the furnace."

Is it any wonder that people have trouble getting back into the groove?

"It's like coming into a football game," said Nick Coleman, a columnist for the *St. Paul Pioneer Press.* "You say 'Me? Go in there? I'll get hurt, I'm not ready.' One day, you're steeped in personal enrichment and the next day you're back in the trenches."

Coleman, 37, remembers his year at the University of Michigan as a time of "extraordinary personal growth" and is still drawing on the benefits of his 1979 sabbatical.

"There's a piece of Ann Arbor that's still in me. I liked who I was there and I try to get back to that whenever I can. Many people who take a leave think it's going to be a great experience for nine months and then it will be over, but it's never over because it changes you.

"The biggest frustration, though, is that nobody else changes. You want to tell people all about your experiences and they say, 'Hey, I'd love to hear about it, let's do lunch sometime.' But nobody really wants to know how rewarding your life has become, how your horizons have expanded, while they were back at the office, bashing their brains out. All of a sudden, all the reasons that caused you to take a leave in the first place come rushing back."

Ah, yes. Telephones still ring, deadlines still loom, bills still arrive, children still need orthodontia, two-hour commutes still take two hours, and difficult people are still difficult. Trying to settle back into an old routine is like trying to force your foot into a shoe that no longer fits. Everyone experiences some postleave blues. Rather than fight it—which only exacerbates the situation—allow yourself the right to feel bad. After all, this has been the object of your time, energy, and finances, not just for the duration of your leave, but perhaps for years before your departure. The realization that it really is over is bound to leave you feeling empty and let down.

Judy Stoia experienced that same "postpartum depression" after she returned from a Neiman Fellowship at Harvard, even though she never left Boston.

"You've had this stimulating year and then you return and things are pretty much the way you left them, which is why such a high percentage of Neiman Fellows—about 60 percent—leave their jobs after their first year. It certainly was true of my class." (At the time of her leave, Stoia was at WGBH-TV, the public broadcasting station in Boston. Now she's an executive producer at WCVB, an ABC affiliate.)

"It's not so much a reflection on the office as it is on the individual. My advice to people who are reentering is to sit down while you are still feeling refreshed, look down the road a couple years, and ask 'Is this where I really want to be?' "

Stoia's advice is sound. A sabbatical almost always inspires some career decisions because, for many, it's the first time in years that there is time to reflect, not just react. Before you jump back on the treadmill, do something with those insights; jot them down and discuss them with your supervisor. Don't just let them fall through the cracks.

Such introspection led Fern Zipursky to the conclusion that she liked social work, but what she really wanted was to be her own boss, so she set up her own counseling practice.

Steve Perry, a commercial artist, followed a similar entrepreneurial path and hung out his own shingle. "I had to do it gradually because I was terrified of life without a steady paycheck. I found out that I could get along okay. When I returned, I had to decide whether to return to my old life or throw myself out of the nest completely. After three months on a sailboat, I found that I was more of a risk-taker than I had ever given myself credit for. If I could survive by my wits on the high seas, I could survive anything."

Not everyone seeks new fortunes. Before his sabbatical, Gibson Anderson, an engineer with Rolm Corporation, had no desire to leave. But while he was away, he realized that what he liked best was talking to young people who were eager to get into the business. Today, he's the company's director of human resources.

And some people, much to their surprise, don't change a thing. When Stephen Feinstein, 41, a history professor at the University of Wisconsin-River Falls, departed for a sabbatical at Tel Aviv University, he was certain a career change was in the cards. Salaries were frozen, admissions were down, and the number of colleagues fleeing academia for the corporate world was at an all-time high. Feinstein recalls boarding the plane for Tel Aviv feeling "fatigued and cynical." Seven months later, he returned with a fresh perspective.

While he was gone, there was a change of administration, so he experienced a surge of optimism that wasn't there before. He remembered why he entered education in the first place. Once he realized that he wasn't stuck in teaching—that this was his choice—he immediately felt more positive. In fact, he was downright excited about returning to the classroom.

Feinstein was fortunate, but he also took some steps to help his own cause. He returned and spoke to groups and organizations on the Middle East. Eventually, his expertise brought an offer to host a local weekly TV show on foreign affairs.

Most people returning to the real world need another project to get interested in. It doesn't need to be a TV show, but it could be starting a quilt, finishing a basement, putting in a garden, or taking piano lessons—something, anything, that keeps the momentum going and helps you think of yourself as having a multifaceted life.

"It was the loss of adventure that was the hardest to take," said Fern Zipursky. "When we were traveling, every day was different; even looking out the window was exciting. When you're deciding whether your next stop should be India or Thailand, it's difficult to come back to the same humdrum existence. I needed something more."

Other tips to minimize the discomfort of reentry:

• Leave yourself plenty of time after you get home before returning to work. Not only may you be faced with jet lag and climate differences, but cultural ones as well. (One day you're lingering over café au lait in some French bistro and the next you're gulping instant coffee in a leaky paper cup, trying to catch the 7:55.) If you've been away for a few months, returning on a Sunday with the idea of starting bright and early Monday morning is just asking for trouble.

• The very first week back at the office, you may want to turn in your resignation, but don't make any major life changes immediately. Give yourself time to get your land legs back. If, after a few months, you're still feeling like a square peg in a round hole, then start taking steps to change the situation. But for right now, the same advice given to the newly divorced and the newly widowed holds true for the newly returned: Don't do anything drastic.

• Hold on to your "free spirit" mindset—at least as much as possible within the confines of a 9-to-5 world. That means keeping the sailboat stocked up or the camper gassed up, so weekend getaways can be pulled together at a moment's notice.

• Resist the temptation to be a born-again leave-taker. It's easy to overwhelm people with slides, travelogues, and your solution for peace in the Middle East or world hunger. It is impossible to condense six months into a two-minute exchange over the water cooler, so don't even try. Come up with a short, upbeat answer to satisfy the co-worker who is just trying to be polite and you'll both feel better. Save the really long stories for people who've had similar experiences. (One of the fringe benefits of writing this book was the sheer delight of finding people who were as awed by a Jerusalem sunset as I was or who could share my enthusiasm for a little café near the Nice train station.)

• Keep favorite photos out where you can see them, not buried in some album. Surround yourself with souvenirs you picked up on your trip. Such reminders can keep a special place indelibly etched in your mind and your heart. On my desk, I have a photograph of a gondola gliding by our window in Venice. On days when all hell is breaking loose, it offers a giant dose of escapism. It is also tangible proof that our leave wasn't a dream. It really happened—and it may very well happen again.

IF YOU'RE RETURNING
FROM ABROAD

People who are returning after a long period out of the country have to make even greater adjustments. Ironically, reverse culture shock (returning home) can strike harder than when you first left the United States to go to a foreign country. When you go overseas, you expect a new language, new customs, new people. Quite simply, you anticipated homesickness and days when you would feel truly out of place in your new surroundings. However, few people expect to feel like a stranger in their own country. Returning expatriates don't make the same allowances that they did when they went overseas—after all, this is home, isn't it?

According to health experts, reentry shock can be even more acute than the culture shock you experienced when you arrived in your new surroundings. Said Dr. Jerome Bergheim: "The fact that it's unexpected means that it hits harder. You may think, 'Gosh, I've just had this wonderful once-in-a-lifetime trip and I'm feeling sad. What's wrong with me?' "

Jeff Langer experienced the first throes of culture shock when he went from India to Thailand. "Within minutes of arriving in Bangkok, I sensed things were very different. I had just come from a place where electricity does not exist, and within minutes I had stepped into an air-conditioned airport, taken an escalator, and had a Coke with ice—three things I hadn't experienced for quite a while. It was a good way to ease back into the United States."

But even that transition did not prepare him for the feelings of alienation he would experience once he returned to New York, the place he had lived his entire life.

"The one thing you can count on in New York is change; buildings are always going up and coming down, but after a year the impact of those changes was far greater. A West Side neighborhood that I liked a lot had died. I just didn't feel like I belonged there anymore; in fact, the only place where I really felt comfortable was Chinatown."

Usually, the longer the trip, the more profound the feelings of being out of sync. Meg and Don Argosi of Denver spent two years traveling around South America and Europe. When they returned in 1986, they were struck with the size of the houses, the cars, and the shopping malls. "Everything seemed to be carried to extremes," said Meg Argosi. "Even food seemed to be super salty, sweet, or greasy. Because the news is overwhelmingly local, we're not aware of how isolated our country is. When we were traveling, we didn't feel as out of touch from the United States as we now feel from the rest of the world."

The wealth and wastefulness of the United States is something that can be discomforting. Said Don Argosi: "Just today I was throwing out a pair of old blue jeans and I thought, 'The zipper is still good. Wouldn't the people of Bolivia like to have these?' "

Catherine Watson, travel editor of the *Minneapolis Star Tribune,* recalls feeling that there was simply too much "stuff" in America. "Complaining to family and friends or, worse, attacking them for being part of it also seems to be part of reentry shock. But it isn't very productive. A better approach is to learn from your feelings of guilt and anger and use them to guide your own behavior and decisions in the future. You are in the unusual position of belonging to two cultures, and although that may be uncomfortable now, there is a strength in it that you can put to good use."

PLANNING YOUR NEXT GETAWAY

When's the best time to start planning your next personal leave? While the memories are still fresh and the motivation is still strong.

With a bank account that is hemorrhaging red ink, it may seem downright foolish to think about your next "time out." But putting away a little each month is not only building a nest egg, but is a way of acknowledging that this doesn't have to be regarded as a once-in-a-lifetime fantasy.

It does come around again. Ask people at Rolm Computers, McDonald's, or any of the other companies that offer paid sabbaticals as a benefit.

"We're just starting to see people who are coming up for their second leave," said Larry Chamberlin, a Rolm vice president. (The company initiated the benefit in 1974 and employees are eligible every six years of service.)

But for most of us, there will be no corporate angels. Fern and Arnie Zipursky set up a separate "getaway" account, with a tentative date of 1990. "Just knowing that we're making plans has helped me get back into my old routine," Fern said. "The hum-drum doesn't seem so meaningless because we have a goal."

If your finances are so strapped that you cannot even put away a token amount, there are dozens of other ways to lay the ground-work for your next sabbatical, thus keeping the dream alive:

- Send away for information on cultural exchange and inter-national programs.
- Learn a foreign language.
- Speak to local organizations (you never know when they might need a tour guide).
- Continually look for ways to push your benefits to the maximum. If you qualified for a personal leave this go-round, scout out what it takes to be eligible for an educational, social service, or loaned executive leave.
- Investigate companies with offices abroad. The U.S. State Department estimates that some two million Americans work for companies with branches overseas. If you are interested in living in a specific country, talk to the consulate or national tourist office. If you're open to just about anyone who will issue a paycheck, there are several books on the subject of foreign employment, such as *The Dictionary of American Firms Operating in Foreign Countries* (World Trade Academy Press). For others, check the bibliography.

Said Mark Ugowski, already squirreling away money for his next sojourn: "Nothing is once in a lifetime. All I know is that there's a big party out there and I want to dance."

June 22, 1985

It is our last day in Cannes. I rented a dinghy, rowed as far as I dared, then settled down with Growing Up *by Russell Baker. For about an hour, it was just me and Baker, bobbing in the water. Years from now I'm going to carry this afternoon with me, like a mental snapshot: the sun dancing on the sea, the rough-hewn wood of the oars, the stillness of the air, the renewal of the spirit.*

EPILOGUE

Advance one year. The sabbatical is long over, but like the twist of a kaleidoscope, it altered the pattern of everything else in our lives.

We never moved back into our house in Minneapolis. Instead, we moved to Chicago, and turned from suburbanites to urban dwellers. When we returned to the United States in August, David took a new job with a Loop architectural firm. I took the features editor position that was offered just a week before our departure—the one that almost caused me to cancel the trip. Work—and life—go on.

But what was most astounding to me was how quickly it all can stop. One day, work is demanding every ounce of time, energy, and attention. The next day, it's gone. The switch is just flicked off. And do you know what happens? *Absolutely nothing.*

For the first month, I expected the job police to grab me by the collar, brandish a badge, and say, "Hey, shouldn't you be at the office?" or "It's Tuesday at 10:30. Don't you have a staff meeting?" It never happened.

Even months into my leave, my thoughts would still drift back to what I would be doing if I were at home. If it were an ordinary Thursday, for example, I would think about how I would have a story due. Or how, at lunch, I would try to squeeze a day's worth of sun into thirty minutes. Or how I'd be sitting in some meeting, stifling a scream while grown men and women debated the merits of the theme "City Looks" versus "Artful Dressing" for the fall fashion section.

But that very same Thursday was filled instead with colors and music and gelati in Venice's San Marco square or with history at Chambourd, one of France's most stunning chateaus, or with unabashed voyeurism on the French Riviera. Each day was like a blank check and we decided how it should be spent. And the only reason that I was here and my co-workers were there was because I *took* it—and that never stopped being a kick.

There have been more substantive benefits, as well. I can say unequivocally that I take more chances than I ever did before. There is a certain ripple effect to risk-taking. Once you've broken the rules, with good results, you're more apt to do it again and again.

I've also learned some patience. I actually stop for yellow lights; I no longer sit on the edge of my chair as if I'm waiting for a starting gun to go off; I don't chafe when someone is telling a long, drawn-out story or when lines are achingly slow—a lesson learned in Europe, where people refuse to be rushed.

I'm better at sweeping away life's clutter. (In the larger scheme of things, no one really cares whether you make your own spaghetti sauce or you spoon it from a jar.) We regard anxiety as this external element that moves in on our lives, but we're the ones who usually roll out the welcome mats. Even on a kibbutz, I found myself making lists. If I were shipwrecked on a remote island, I would start a list with "polish coconuts, sweep beach . . ."

That relentless pursuit of perfection has eased. Every editor barks out the same demands: "Make it short, make it fast, and make it sing." But there are days when you have to settle for just "short."

Most of all, I learned that no job is worth sacrificing your health, your relationships, or your life for.

Now that kind of thinking will certainly put me in the middle of the pack of my profession, which is okay. Because life isn't a sprint; it's a marathon.

September 10, 1985

I've been back a little over a month and people keep telling me that what we did was "gutsy" or "risky."

What risk? I had a job to return to, I was with loved ones, we had a return ticket if things went terribly wrong. We had left our home in the hands of a capable manager. If the leave put us in a financial hole, we had another thirty years to climb out.

But if I had stayed, I'd run the risk of growing stale; of resenting something I had always loved. The savings account would be full, but the spirit would be bankrupt. It seemed to me that the course of action was not nearly as risky as the course of inaction.

APPENDIX

Fellowships and Grants

Architecture

Senior Fellowships
(A stipend of $7,000 plus housing is awarded to outstanding landscape architects and horticulturists.)

Assistant Director
Center for Studies in Landscape Architecture
Dumbarton Oaks
1703 32nd St. N.W.
Washington, D.C. 20007

Rotch Traveling Scholarship
(A stipend of $13,000 for eight months of foreign travel is awarded to architects under 35 who received their architecture training from a Massachusetts school.)

Norman C. Fletcher
46 Brattle St.
Cambridge, Mass. 02138

Arts

Artists' Project Grants
(Funds for Connecticut artists to set aside time to work.)

Connecticut Commission for the Arts
340 Capitol Ave.
Hartford, Conn. 06106

Eben Demarest Trust
(Funds to an artist who "wishes to concentrate . . . without having to depend on the sale of work or outside jobs.")

Eben Demarest Fund
4601 Bayard St., Apt. 807
Pittsburgh, Penn. 15213

George A. and Eliza Gardner Howard Foundation
(Seeks to aid the personal development of promising individuals at the crucial middle stages of their career. Fellowships are offered for independent projects in literary criticism, art history, foreign language studies, musicology, theater, and film criticism. Applicants should be between 30 and 40 years old.)

Box 1867
Brown University
Providence, R.I. 12912

Helen Wurlitzer Foundation of New Mexico
(Residence grants in Taos, New Mexico, are offered in the fields of writing, painting, sculpture, musical composition, and choreography. Grants are usually for a three-month period, which may be lengthened up to one year.)

P.O. Box 545
Taos, N.M. 87571

The Millay Colony for the Arts, Inc.
(Provides room, board, and work space for qualified writers, composers, and visual artists while they complete projects.)

Steepletop
Austerlitz, N.Y. 12017

Business

It is probably no coincidence that business fellowships are, well, all business. These programs will not set you off the career treadmill, but they will set you out of the office. Virtually every well-regarded graduate school of business offers some sort of continuing education. Here is just a sampling:

Sloan Program
(Nine-month program for middle managers with a minimum of eight years experience. A masters of science in management is awarded at completion of the program.)

Graduate School of Business
Stanford University
Stanford, Calif. 94305-5015

Alfred P. Sloan Program
(One-year masters program for middle managers with a minimum of ten years experience.)

Massachusetts Institute of Technology
50 Memorial Drive, E52-126
Cambridge, Mass. 02139

Advanced Management Program/Program for Management Development
(Harvard has several programs for business executives. One of the best known is the Advanced Management Program, for those with broad experience in top-management positions. The program brings together a diverse group of senior executives from every important sector of the world's economies. Typical participants have twenty years of experience and are at the vice-president level or higher. For those in middle-management ranks with ten years in the work force, Harvard offers a twelve-week program for management development.)

Administrative Director
Glass Hall
Harvard Business School
Cambridge, Mass. 02163

International Business Operations
(Four-week international business program in London is designed for MBA students, but eligible professionals are also accepted. The program is offered by Southern Illinois University in cooperation with Danbury Park Management Centre.)

Study Abroad Programs
Southern Illinois University
Carbondale, Ill. 62901

Small-Scale Enterprises in Developing Countries
(Two-month program examines the problems of small businesses in Third World countries.)

Malcolm Harper
Cranfield School of Management
Cranfield, Bedford MK43 OAL, England

Environment

American Alpine Club
(Grants to support research and mountaineering in alpine environments.)

113 East 90th St.
New York, N.Y. 10028

The American Museum of Natural History
(Grants to support research in North America on wildlife conservation and natural history.)

Central Park West at 79th St.
New York, N.Y. 10024

Food and Nutrition

American Dietetic Association
(Sponsors five different programs, with different purposes and eligibility.)

430 North Michigan Ave.
Chicago, Ill. 60611

American Home Economics Association Foundation
(Sponsors eighteen different programs, with funds ranging from $1,000
to $5,000. Eligibility varies depending on the program.)

2010 Massachusetts Ave. N.W.
Washington, D.C. 20036

International Association of Cooking Schools
(A scholarship to a recognized cooking school is available if you have
demonstrated an interest in a professional food career.)

1001 Connecticut Ave., Suite 800
Washington, D.C. 20036

Health

New York Life Foundation Scholarship Program for Women in the
Health Professions
(Scholarships ranging from $250 to $1,000 will be awarded to women 25
years or older who are within two years of graduating in the health-care
field.)

Business and Professional Women's Foundation
2012 Massachusetts Ave. N.W.
Washington, D.C. 20036

Journalism

Walter Bagehot Fellowship
(Tuition and stipend for experienced business journalists to study at
Columbia University.)

Mary Bralove
Graduate School of Journalism
Columbia University
New York, N.Y. 10027

William Benton Fellowships in Broadcasting
(Tuition and stipend for broadcasters to study at the University of Chicago.)

Director, Benton Fellowships
University of Chicago, Room 501
5801 South Ellis Ave.
Chicago, Ill. 60637

Vannevar Bush Fellowships
(Stipend for writers and broadcasters with at least three years' experience
in reporting health and science to study at MIT.)

    Vannevar Bush Fellowship Program, E40-373
    Massachusetts Institute of Technology
    Cambridge, Mass. 02139

Carnegie-Mellon Fellowships
(Tuition and stipend for experienced journalists to attend in-residence
executive programs.)

    Professor Bernard P. Goldsmith
    Carnegie-Mellon University, Box 10
    Pittsburgh, Pa. 15213

Congressional Fellowship Program
(Provides $16,000 stipend for journalists to work nine months on the
staffs of House or Senate members.)

    American Political Science Association
    1527 New Hampshire Ave., N.W.
    Washington, D.C. 20036

Gannett Fellowships in Asian Studies for Journalists
(Provides tuition and fees, transportation, and a $15,000 stipend for
journalists to study at the University of Hawaii.)

    Gannett Fellowship Committee
    Center for Asian and Pacific Studies
    University of Hawaii
    1890 East-West Road
    Honolulu, Hawaii 96822

Journalists in Residence Fellowships
(Provides tuition and $2,000 monthly stipend for liberal arts study.)

    Graham Hovey, Director
    University of Michigan
    2072 Frieze Building
    Ann Arbor, Mich. 48109

Kellogg Fellowship Program
(Provides funds for self-directed study.)

Kellog Foundation
400 North Ave.
Battle Creek, Mich. 49016

John S. Knight Fellowships for Professional Journalists
(Provides $20,000 stipend and other funds for mid-career journalists to "broaden and deepen their understanding of the issues and trends shaping the nation and the world.")

Director, Knight Fellowship Program
Department of Communication
Stanford University
Stanford, Calif. 94305-2069

Macy Fellowships in Science Broadcast Journalism
(For science writers who wish to move into science broadcast journalism. WGBH-Boston will train fellows, who will receive a $25,000 stipend.)

44 East 64th St.
New York, N.Y. 10021

Edward R. Murrow Fellowship
(Funds for journalists covering foreign stories.)

Council on Foreign Relations
58 East 68th St.
New York, N.Y. 10021

National Press Foundation
(Provides funds for projects that contribute to improving the quality of journalism.)

1160 National Press Building
Washington, D.C. 20045

Nieman Fellowships
(Provides $12,000 stipend for nondegree study at Harvard.)

Program Director, Nieman Foundation
Harvard University
Walter Lippmann House
One Francis Ave.
Cambridge, Mass. 02138

Alicia Patterson Foundation Fellowships
(One-year grants of $25,000 to pursue independent projects.)

   Helen McMaster Coulson, Executive Director
   The Alicia Patterson Foundation
   655 Fifteenth St. N.W., Suite 320
   Washington, D.C. 20005

Eugene C. Pulliam Fellowship
(Provides $10,000 for travel and study for editorial writers.)

   Pulliam Fellowship
   Sigma Delta Chi Foundation
   53 West Jackson, Suite 731
   Chicago, Ill. 60604

Rotary Foundation Educational Program
(Funds are provided for one year of study abroad; however, the scholarship is primarily "ambassadorial.")

   Rotary International Foundation
   1600 Ridge Ave.
   Evanston, Ill. 60201

Ellen B. Scripps Fellowships
(Funds for graduate studies.)

   Scripps Howard Foundation
   1100 Central Trust Tower
   Cincinnati, Ohio 45202

W. Eugene Smith Memorial Fund
(A $15,000 grant for photographers for "work in progress of a documentary photojournalism project.")

   Smith Fund, International Center of Photography
   1130 Fifth Ave.
   New York, N.Y. 10028

Louis S. St. Laurent Fellowships
(Canadian journalists are provided funds for one year of law school.)

   Stephen Hanson
   Canadian Bar Association, Suite 1700
   130 Albert
   Ottawa, Ontario K1P 5G4
   Canada

White House Fellowships
(Stipends up to $43,000 a year for work with officials in Washington "to provide gifted and highly motivated Americans with some firsthand experience in the process of governing the nation.")

President's Commission on White House Fellowships
712 Jackson Place N.W.
Washington, D.C. 20503

Yale Law School Fellowship in Law for Journalists
(Program provides tuition for one year of study leading to a master of studies-in-law degree.)

Yale Law School
401A Yale Station
New Haven, Conn. 06520

Law

Law is about as straight-laced as business. There are plenty of programs for foreign lawyers who want to study here, but it's slim picking if you want to go the opposite direction.

Harvard recognizes the need for continuing legal education with a two-week "Program of Instruction." Taught by the law school faculty every June, its primary goal is to offer an overview of the subject. It's geared for attorneys, but a limited number of non-lawyers is admitted.

More extensive is the year-long continuing education program, designed for those who have practiced several years and would now like to teach. A Masters of Law is awarded at the end of the program. For information write:

Graduate Programs
Harvard Law School
Cambridge, MA 02138

University of Exeter Center for European Legal Studies
(Study for lawyers who are interested in European community law.)

University of Exeter
Amory Building
Rennes Drive
Exeter, England

Library Science

SLA Scholarships
(Funds for graduate study for people interested in "the theory and practice of library or information science.")

Special Libraries Association, Scholarship Committee
1700 18th St. N.W.
Washington, D.C. 20009

Music

San Francisco Opera Center
(Young professional singers, between the ages of 20 and 34, interested in career development opportunities.)

War Memorial Opera House
San Francisco, Calif. 94102

Sinfonia Foundation
(Research assistance grants for work in American music or music education.)

10600 Old State Rd.
Evansville, Ind. 47711

ZBS Foundation
(an artist-in-residence program allows one New York artist each month to experiment with the possibilities available in audio and sound production. The visiting artist will have all technical facilities as well as a staff available at ZBS Studios, located in upstate New York.)

RD No. 1
Fort Edward, N.Y. 12828

Political and Social Sciences

Council for European Studies
(Awards for short stays in Europe to assist in development of dissertations.)

1404 International Affairs Building
Columbia University
New York, N.Y. 10027

Institute of Current World Affairs Inc.
(One or two long-term fellowships are awarded each year to individuals from varied academic and professional backgrounds to observe and study foreign cultures.)

Wheelock House
4 West Wheelock St.
Hanover, N.H. 03755

James McKeen Cattell Fund
(Supplements sabbatical allowances to psychologists.)

Dr. Robert Thorndike, secretary/treasurer
James McKeen Cattell Fund
Box 219, 525 West 120th St.
New York, N.Y. 10027

Sidney Harman Fellowship
(To study ways to improve the quality of the working environment by creating projects in the public and private sector.)

John F. Kennedy School of Government
Harvard University
79 Boylston St.
Cambridge, Mass. 02138

Resources

There are some outstanding organizations that will offer you more than pamphlets and brochures: a warm, reassuring voice on the other end of the phone. The extensive network, more than anything else, will convince you that taking time off—particularly for travel—can be a viable option in career planning.

Organizations fall into two categories: those that serve as a clearing-house for information on opportunities abroad and those that help people find alternatives to the traditional forty-hour work week.

Travel

AFS International
313 East 43rd St.
New York, N.Y. 10017

Offers intercultural programs for adults, mostly during the summer months. Application for deadline is April 1.

Council on International Educational Exchange
205 East 42nd St.
New York, N.Y. 10017

There isn't anything this organization (which has been around for forty years) doesn't do—from arranging work permits to car rentals to publishing books considered authoritative in their field. In 1985, they helped 250,000 people with their travel plans.

Experiment in International Living
Kipling Road
Brattleboro, Vt. 05301

A private, nonprofit organization that has promoted international exchange programs since its founding in 1932.

Institute for International Education (IIE)
809 United Nations Plaza
New York, N.Y. 10017

Information on studying and teaching abroad, including U.S. college-sponsored programs abroad, academic year and vacation study abroad. In addition, the IIE operates an information center (at the above address) open Tuesday, Wednesday, and Thursday from 10 A.M. to 4 P.M.

International Employment Hotline
P.O. Box 6170
McLean, Va. 22106

A year's subscription ($26) to the hotline will get you periodic listings of international opportunities.

Mobility International USA
P.O. Box 3551
Eugene, Or. 97403

Information on work camps and accommodations for the disabled traveler.

Overseas Development Network (ODN)
P.O. Box 2306
Stanford, Calif.

A consortium that concentrates on Third World development. A catalog ($15) lists short-term opportunities, and a computer database matches interns with internships.

Peace Corps
Washington, D.C. 20526
(800) 424-8580

Twenty-five years later it's still thriving. Sixty countries.

Service Civil International USA
Route 2, Box 506
Innisfree Village
Crozet, Va. 22931

Organizes workcamps and recruits volunteers.

Transcentury Foundation
1724 Kalorama Road, N.W.
Washington, D.C.

Recruits qualified people for all kinds of employment. Also publishes *Job Opportunities Bulletin* providing information on overseas jobs. A six-month subscription costs $15.

University of Michigan International Center
603 E. Madison
Ann Arbor, Mich. 48109-1370

Another database worth mentioning; ferrets out study/work/travel abroad opportunities.

USSTS
William Sloane House
356 West 34th St.
New York, N.Y. 10001

Publishes annual *Working Abroad* directory.

World Trade Academy Press
50 East 42nd St.
New York, N.Y. 10017

Puts out numerous publications for foreign job seekers, including lists of American companies that operate abroad. If you are interested in a specific field, be sure and ask if there is an appropriate publication (example: *Construction Employment Guide in the National and International Field*).

Volunteers for Peace
Belmont, Vt. 05730

Placement in work camps, primarily in Europe. The *International Workcamp Directory* is available for a $6 donation.

Work

(These organizations are primarily resources for women, but they will help men, too.)

Work/Life Options
5004 West Tierra Buena
Glendale, Ariz. 85306

New Ways to Work
149 Ninth St.
San Francisco, Calif. 94103

Flexible Career Associates
Box 6701
Santa Barbara, Calif. 93111

Innovative Career Options
School of Business
Metropolitan State College
1006 Eleventh St.
Denver, Colo. 80204

Division of Women's Programs
Alternative Working Arrangements Project
Drake University
Des Moines, Iowa 50311

Work Options Limited
645 Boylston St.
Boston, Mass. 02116

Adult Career Exploration Center
Memorial Hall
Glassboro State College
Glassboro, N.J. 08028

Workshare
311 East 50th St.
New York, N.Y. 10022

Flexible Ways to Work
YWCA
1111 S.W. Tenth St.
Portland, Oregon 97205

Work Time Options
966 Summer Place
Pittsburgh, Pa. 15243

Focus
509 Tenth Ave. E.
Seattle, Wash. 98102

BIBLIOGRAPHY

Foreign Jobs, Foreign Study, and Travel

The number of noteworthy travel books is so vast that they could fill another volume. Therefore, our intent is to emphasize books that concentrate on work and study abroad, rather than those written for the tourist. The first place to start is the consulate embassy, or tourist office. They can put you in touch with the right people and—best of all—their services are free.

Anthony, Rebecca, and Gerald Rae, *Educators' Passport to International Jobs: How to Find and Enjoy Employment Abroad* (Princeton, N.J.: Peterson's Guides, 1984).

Campbell, Scott, and Johnston, William Ivers, *Let's Go: The Budget Guide to Europe* (New York: St. Martin's Press, 1986). Updated annually. One of the best compendiums for the budget traveler.

Casewit, Curtis, *Foreign Jobs: The Most Popular Countries* (New York: Monarch Press, 1984).

Council on International Educational Exchange, *Work, Study, Travel Abroad* (New York: St. Martin's Press, 1986). A *must* for anyone who is looking for all the names and addresses of foreign programs—from studying art in Florence to being a nanny in London.

Directory of American Firms Operating in Foreign Countries (New York: World Trade Academy Press; write to the publisher for more information).

Eisenberg, Gerson G. *Learning Vacations: The All-Season Guide to Educational Travel* (Princeton, N.J.: Peterson's Guides, 1987).

Griffith, Susan, *Summer Jobs in Britain 1987* (Cincinnati, Ohio: Writer's Digest Books, 1979).

Howard, Edrice *Vacation Study Abroad* (New York: IIE, 1987).

Kepler, John Z., Kepler, Phyllis J., Gaither, Orville D., Gaither, Margaret L., *Americans Abroad: A Handbook for Living and Working Overseas* (New York: Praeger Publishers, 1983).

Kocher, E., *International Jobs: Where They Are and How to Get Them* (New York: Addison-Wesley, 1983).

Kohls, L. Robert, *Survival Kit for Overseas Living* (Yarmouth, Maine: Intercultural Press, 1984).

Novik, Jack D., *World Almanac's Legal Guide for American Travelers in Western Europe 1986* (New York: World Almanac Publications, 1986).

UNESCO, *Study Abroad: International Scholarships, International Courses* (New York: Unipub, 1986). A directory of financial aid available to those studying abroad. To order: write 1180 Avenue of the Americas, New York, N.Y. 10036.

Watson, Catherine, *Travel Basics* (Minneapolis, Minn.: Minneapolis Star & Tribune Co., 1984).

Wharton, John, *Jobs in Japan: The Complete Guide to Living and Working in the Land of Rising Opportunity* (rev. ed., Denver, Colo.: Global Press, 1986).

Grants, Fellowships, and Other Money Sources

Names and addresses of other financial resources can be found in Chapter 4. Several of the publications listed below, such as the *Annual Register of Grant Support,* are massive compendiums that can be found in the reference section of your library.

A Casebook of Grant Proposals in the Humanities (Neal-Schuman Publishers, Inc., 1983).

Annual Register of Grant Support (Chicago, Ill.: Marquis/Macmillan Directory Division, 1986).

Directory of Financial Aids for International Activities (compiled by the University of Minnesota's International Programs Office; covers opportunities for travel, research, study, and teaching overseas. To order, write to the office at 201 Nolte West, 315 Pillsbury Drive S.E., Minneapolis, Minn. 55455).

Fellowship Guide for Western Europe (compiled by the Council for European Studies at Columbia University, New York). To order, write to the council at 1509 International Affairs Building, Columbia University, New York, N.Y. 10027.

Foundation Directory, Loren Renz, ed. (New York: Foundation Center, 1986).

Grants and Awards Available to American Writers, John Monroe, ed. (New York: PEN American Center, 1986).

The Grants Register 1987–1989, George Walsh, ed. (New York: St. Martin's Press, 1986).

Lesko, Matthew, *Getting Yours: The Complete Guide to Government Money* (rev. ed., New York: Penguin Books, 1982).

————, *Information USA* (New York: Penguin Books, 1986).

Lurie, Joseph, *The Directory of Financial Aid for American Undergraduates Interested in Overseas Study and Travel* (Garden City, N.Y.: Adelphi University Press, 1985).

Margolin, Judith, *The Individual's Guide to Grants* (New York: Plenum Press, 1985).

Porter, Sylvia, *Sylvia Porter's New Money Book for the '80s* (New York: Avon Books, 1980).

Scholarships, Fellowships, Grants, and Loans (New York: Macmillan, 1986).

Smith, Craig, and Skjei, Eric, *Getting Grants: A Creative Guide to the Grants System* (New York: Harper & Row, 1983).

Work and Goal-Setting

Anderson, Nancy, *Work with Passion: How to Do What You Love for a Living* (New York: Carroll & Graf Publishers, Inc., and Mill Valley, Calif.: Whatever Publishing, Inc., 1984).

Blotnik, Srully, *The Corporate Steeplechase: Predictable Crises in a Business Career* (New York: Penguin Books, 1984).

————, *Otherwise Engaged: The Private Lives of Successful Career Women* (New York: Penguin Books, 1986).

Bolles, Richard Nelson, *What Color Is Your Parachute?* (Berkeley, Calif.: Ten Speed Press, 1985).

————, *The Three Boxes of Life And How to Get Out of Them* (Berkeley, Calif.: Ten Speed Press, 1983).

Cohen, Herb, *You Can Negotiate Anything* (New York: Bantam Books, 1982).

Deal, Terrence E., and Kennedy, Allen A., *Corporate Cultures: The Rites and Rituals of Corporate Life* (Reading, Mass.: Addison-Wesley, 1982).

Drucker, Peter, *Management: Tasks, Responsibilities, Practices* (New York: Harper & Row Publishers, 1974).

Harragan, Betty Lehan, *Games Mother Never Taught You: Corporate Gamesmanship for Women* (New York: Warner Books, 1978).

Kanter, Rosabeth Moss, *Men and Women of the Corporation* (New York: Basic Books, 1979).

Kennedy, Marilyn Moats, *Office Politics: Seizing Power, Wielding Clout* (New York: Warner, 1981).

Lee, Patricia, *The Complete Guide to Job Sharing* (New York: Walker & Co., 1983).

Levering, Robert; Moskowitz, Michael; and Katz, Michael; *The 100 Best Companies to Work for in America* (Reading, Mass.: Addison-Wesley, 1984).

McCormack, Mark H., *What They Don't Teach You at Harvard Business School* (New York: Bantam Books, 1985).

Mackoff, Barbara, *Leaving the Office Behind* (New York: Dell Books, 1986).

Marks, Linda, and Feidyn, Karen, *Negotiating Time: New Scheduling Options in the Legal Profession* (New Ways to Work, 149 Ninth St., San Francisco, Calif. 94103, 1986).

Medley, H. Anthony, *Sweaty Palms: The Neglected Art of Being Interviewed* (Berkeley, Calif.: Ten Speed Press, 1984).

Naisbitt, John, and Aburdene, Patricia, *Re-Inventing the Corporation* (New York: Warner Books, 1985).

Olmsted, Barney and Smith, Suzanne, *The Job Sharing Handbook* (Berkeley, Calif.: Ten Speed Press, 1983).

Opportunities Abroad for Teachers (Washington, D.C.: Department of Health, Education and Welfare, 1985).

Patla, Don, *Getting the Most Out of Your Benefits* (New York: Dell Books, 1984).

Peters, Thomas J., and Waterman, Robert H., *In Search of Excellence: Lessons from America's Best-Run Companies* (New York: Harper & Row, 1982).

Robbins, Paula I., *Successful Midlife Career Change: Self-Understanding and Strategies for Action* (New York: Amacom, 1980).

Sher, Barbara, and Gottlieb, Annie, *Wishcraft: How to Get What You Really Want* (New York: Ballantine Books, 1983).

Talley, Madelon DeVoe, *Career Hang Gliding: A Personal Guide to Managing Your Career* (New York: E. P. Dutton, 1986).

Toffler, Alvin, *The Adaptive Corporation* (New York: Bantam Books, 1985).

Wheatley, Meg, and Hirsch, Marcie Shore, *Managing Your Maternity Leave* (New York: Houghton-Mifflin, 1983).

Families and Relationships

Bird, Caroline, *The Two-Paycheck Marriage* (New York: Pocket Books, 1982).

Ruben, Harvey L., *Supermarriage: Overcoming the Predictable Crises of Married Life* (New York: Bantam Books, 1986).

Winfield, Fairlee E., *Commuter Marriage: Living Together, Apart* (New York: Columbia University Press, 1985).

Health

Alexander, Joe, *Dare to Change: How to Program Yourself for Success* (New York: New American Library, 1984).

Bridges, William, *Transitions: Making Sense of Life's Changes* (Boston: Addison-Wesley, 1980).

Bureau of National Affairs, *Alcohol and Drugs in the Workplace: Costs, Controls and Controversies* (1986).

Bureau of National Affairs, *VDTs in the Workplace: A Study of the Effects on Employment* (1984).

Freudenberger, Herbert, and Richelson, Geraldine, *Burn-Out* (New York: Bantam, 1981).

Landau, Sol, *Turning Points: Self-Renewal at Midlife* (Far Hills, N.J.: New Horizon Press NJ, 1985).

Mason, L. John, *Guide to Stress Reduction* (Berkeley, Calif.: Celestial Arts, 1985).

Talking to firms that already have formal sabbatical programs is like preaching to the converted. What about other companies? The following all said that a personal leave could be arranged on a case-by-case basis. It is not meant to be an exhaustive list, only to show the diversity of companies that are open to leave proposals, depending on how they are pitched and by whom.

Apple Computer, Inc., Cupertino, Calif.
Atlantic Richfield (oil), Los Angeles, Calif.
Bell Laboratories (research & development for AT&T), Murray Hill, N.J.
Borg-Warner (manufacturing), Chicago, Ill.
Control-Data (computers), Minneapolis, Minn.
Dayton-Hudson (retailing), Minneapolis, Minn.
Doyle Dane Bernbach (advertising), New York, N.Y.
Donnelly Mirrors (rearview mirrors), Holland, Mich.
Exxon Corp. (oil), New York, N.Y.
General Electric (electronics), Fairfield, Conn.
General Mills (food), Minneapolis, Minn.
Gore (makers of Gore-tex), Newark, Del.
Hallmark (greeting cards), Kansas City, Mo.
Hewitt Associates (designs benefit and compensation programs for companies), Lincolnshire, Ill.
Hewlitt Packard (computers), Palo Alto, Calif.
IBM (office equipment), Armonk, N.Y.
Kimberly Clark (paper products), Neenah, Wisc.
Knight-Ridder (newspapers), Miami, Fla.
Leo Burnett (advertising), Chicago, Ill.
Maytag (appliances), Newton, Iowa
Northwestern Mutual Life Insurance Co., Milwaukee, Wisc.
Pitney Bowes (postage meters), Stamford, Conn.
Random House (publishing), New York, N.Y.
3M (tape), St. Paul, Minn.
Wells Fargo (banking), San Francisco, Calif.
Xerox (photocopiers), New York, N.Y.

INDEX